ANTIGRAV

ANTIGRAV

Cosmic Comedies by SF Masters

Edited by PHILIP STRICK

Taplinger Publishing Company / New York

Grateful acknowledgement is made for permission to include the following
copyright material:

Space Rats of the C.C.C. © 1974 by Edward L. Ferman and Barry N.
Malzberg.

How the World Was Saved © 1974 by Seabury Press Inc. New York from
The Cyberiad: Fables from the Cybernetic Age.

It Was Nothing—Really! © 1969 by Sirkay Publishers Corp.; originally appeared in *Sturgeon is Alive and Well* published by G. P. Putnam's Sons, and
reprinted by permission of the author and the E. J. Carnell Agency.

The Glitch © 1974 by James Blish.

Conversation on a Starship in Warpdrive © 1975 by John Brosnan, published
by permission of the author and Michael Bakewell & Associates Ltd.

The Alibi Machine © 1973 by the Mankind Publishing Company; originally
appeared in *Vertex*, Vol. 1 No. 2, and reprinted by permission of the author
and the E. J. Carnell Agency.

Emergency Society © 1975 by Uta Frith.

Look, You Think You've Got Troubles? ©1969 by Damon Knight and
reprinted from *Orbit 5* by permission of the author.

A Delightful Comedic Premise © 1974 by the Mercury Press Inc. First
published in the magazine of *Fantasy and Science Fiction* 1974 and reprinted
by permission of the author.

Trolls © 1975 by Robert Borski, published by permission of the author and
Michael Bakewell & Associates Ltd.

Elephant With Wooden Leg © 1975 by UPD Publishing Corporation, with
first U.S. publication in *Galaxy*.

Planting Time © 1975 by Pete Adams and Charles Nightingale.

By the Seashore © 1973 by UPD Publishing Corporation and reprinted by
permission of the author and his agent Virginia Kidd.

Hardcastle © 1971 by Ron Goulart, originally appeared in *What's Become
of Screwloose?*, published by Charles Scribner's Sons, and reprinted by permission of the author.

The Ergot Show © 1972 by Harry Harrison and reprinted from *Nova 2* by
permission of the author.

For Lizanne who laughs as well

Contents

8 Contents

Introduction

You are holding, I should warn you, an anti-gravity device. Hold on tight! The ground may at any moment disappear from beneath your feet.

The suspension of laws, natural or otherwise, is the prerogative of science fiction. It is the most disrespectful of literatures, taking nothing for granted, no present, past or future stone unturned. It deals with ideas that are on the attack, refusing to accept that the way things are today is any guarantee they'll be like that tomorrow.

Science fiction writers, as Eliot Rosewater reminds us, are the only ones who know what's going on any more. They see that the world is square and flat and made of concrete, its inhabitants tiny, vulnerable, and much given to self-destruction, music, dreams and melancholy. They see that the world might well be a useful place to relinquish in favour of brighter, more seductive planets, sprinkled like treasure islands across an infinite ocean. They see, too, that man may never bother to make the effort to change his life and times unless he's constantly jabbed, kicked and goaded. And they see that when he *does* get out there, skimming gleefully across the stars in an orgy of tourism, he'll try and take his old laws with him, his perpetual fears, instincts and idiocies, heavy around his neck.

So science fiction dares to be impossible, to place the secret of anti-gravity in our hands and fling us out of the dimensions that grow more claustrophobic, more insupportable around us year by year. It dares to ask if the curious rules by which society defines its boundaries are really the rules by which any rational person wants to live. It dares to point out the consequences of those rules, and their alternatives. It dares to lift us off the ground so that there's a chance we'll see more clearly just what we've been standing in.

Yet science fiction is human. It's no more certain of its answers than any of the rest of us. It recognizes that an excessively detached view of the planet might also have its dangers. The Apollo astronauts have taken some strange directions since they returned from the experience of watching us all fall into the sky like a tumbling blue-green marble. Demolish too many principles, and you can get left with nothing more than a severe case of insecurity. Travel too high, and you forget where you started from, and why you left.

The answer is a safety-belt, and few science fiction stories travel without one. The world may be roasted, blown apart, or turned to crystal, but the survivors manage to demonstrate reassuring powers of courage and rehabilitation. They even manage, if a little gloomily at times, to enjoy themselves. Overpopulation and ecological breakdown may render the planetary surface a mile thick all over with starving bodies, but love and ingenuity are still hard at work in an irresistible confidence that life will, no matter what, have been worth the candle. The future may prove to be quite abominable, but science fiction never seems to be in any doubt that there'll *be* one. And one of the most effective ways to make it tolerable, of course, is to subject it to a certain amount of scorn.

Such is the solemnity with which the merits of science fiction are argued and defended these days that one of its greatest talents seems to have been overlooked. Science fiction can indeed be brutal, grim, and fraught with warning. It can indeed be majestic, visionary, resounding with hope and expectation. It can be trivial, ludicrous and banal, populated with dragons and swordsmen on the prowl. But it can also be funny, and it spends a heartening amount of its time being just that. Tears may sometimes be in its eyes, a suggestion of hysteria in its voice, but science fiction resounds with irony and good clear laughter.

We decided it was time to invalidate the notion that science fiction writers, world-famed as the most enthusiastic of party-goers and drinking companions, are only cheerful away from their typewriters. This anthology was planned as a way to show that science fiction is the most irreverent and inventive cabaret in all contemporary writing. Yet I have to admit that in some senses the writers have had the last laugh – they're an uncontrollable race. The stories you are about to encounter are on a rampage, recognizing no limits, no constants, no comforts. If they have anything in common, it's that they're unconventional. They take one look at today and discard it as irrelevant.

On the example of at least some of the evidence that follows, I believe that science fiction is the most exciting and the most important writing to be found anywhere in this world. I'm delighted that some of its greatest showmen are represented in this collection, several of them caught in mid-flight through the surrealistic altitudes that they have increasingly begun to explore. Part of the new function that science fiction has taken upon itself in the past dozen years is that of a literature investigating the whole structure of writing, the whole extent to which style must change to match new themes. Big waves and little, old and new, are pounding the shore in this anthology. Their sound is the most adventurous kind of music.

They confirm, too, one certain thing about the future. We'll need a sense of humour in order to cope with it.

Philip Strick

ANTIGRAV

Space Rats of the C.C.C.
Harry Harrison

That's it, matey, pull up a stool! Sure, use that one. Just dump
old Phrnnx onto the floor to sleep it off. You know that
Krddls can't stand to drink, much less drink *flnnx*; and that
topped off with a smoke of the hellish *krmml* weed. Here, let
me pour you a mug of *flnnx*, oops, sorry about your sleeve.
When it dries you can scrape it off with a knife. Here's to your
health and may your tubeliners never fail you when the
kpnnz hordes are on your tail.

No, sorry, never heard your name before. Too many good
men come and go and the good ones die early, aye! Me? You
never heard of me. Just call me Old Sarge, as good a name as
any. Good men, I say, and the best of them was – well, we'll
call him Gentleman Jax. He had another name, but there's a
little girl waiting on a planet I could name, a little girl that's
waiting and watching the shimmering trails of the deep-
spacers when they come, and waiting for a man. So for her
sake we'll call him Gentleman Jax, he would have liked that,
and she would like that if only she knew, although she must
be getting kind of grey, or bald by now, and arthritic from all
that sitting and waiting but, golly, that's another story and by
Orion it's not for me to tell. That's it, help yourself, a large
one. Sure, the green fumes are normal for good *flnnx*, though
you better close your eyes when you drink or you'll be blind
in a week, ha-ha!, by the sacred name of the Prophet Mrddl!

Yes, I can tell what you're thinking. What's an old space
rat like me doing in a dive like this out here at galaxy's end,
where the rim stars flicker wanly and the tired photons go
slow? I'll tell you what I'm doing, getting drunker than a

Planizzian *pfrdffl*, that's what. They say that drink has the power to dim memories and by Cygnus I have some memories that need dimming. I see you looking at those scars on my hands. Each one is a story matey, aye, and the scars on my back each a story and the scars on my . . . well, that's a different story. Yes, I'll tell you a story, a true one by Mrddl's holy name, though I might change a name or two, that little girl waiting, you know.

You heard tell of the C.C.C.? I can see by the sudden widening of your eyes and the blanching of your space-tanned skin that you have. Well yours truly, Old Sarge here, was one of the first of the Space Rats of the C.C.C., and my buddy then was the man they know as Gentleman Jax. May Great Kramddl curse his name and blacken the memory of the first day when I first set eyes on him . . .

'Graduating class . . . ten-SHUN!'

The sergeant's stentorian voice bellowed forth, cracking like a whiplash across the expectant ears of the mathematically aligned rows of cadets. With the harsh snap of those fateful words a hundred and three incredibly polished bootheels crashed together with a single snap and the eighty-seven cadets of the graduating class snapped to steel-rigid attention. (It should be explained that some of them were from alien worlds, and had different numbers of legs, etc.) Not a breath was drawn, not an eyelid twitched a thousandth of a millilitre as Colonel von Thorax stepped forward, glaring down at them all through the glass monocle in front of his glass eye, close-cropped grey hair stiff as barbed wire, black uniform faultlessly cut and smooth, a *krmml* weed cigarette clutched in the steel fingers of his prosthetic left arm, black gloved fingers of his prosthetic right arm snapping to hatbrim's edge in a perfect salute, motors whining thinly in his prosthetic lungs to power the brobdignagian roar of his harshly bellowed command.

'At ease. And listen to me. You are the hand-picked men –

and hand-picked things, too, of course – from all the civilized worlds of the galaxy. Six million and forty-three cadets entered the first year of training and most of them washed out in one way or another. Some could not toe the mark. Some were expelled and shot for buggery. Some believed the lying commy pinko crying liberal claims that continuous war and slaughter is not necessary and they were expelled, and shot as well. One by one the weaklings fell away through the years, leaving the hard core of the Corps – *you*! The Corpsmen of the first graduating class of the C.C.C.! Ready to spread the benefits of civilization to the stars. Ready at last to find out what the initials C.C.C. stand for!'

A mighty roar went up from the massed throats, a cheer of hoarse masculine enthusiasm that echoed and boomed from the stadium walls. At a signal from von Thorax a switch was thrown and a great shield of imperviomite slid into place above, sealing the stadium from prying eyes and ears and snooping spyish rays. The roaring voices roared on enthusiastically – and many an eardrum was burst that day! – yet were stilled in an instant when the Colonel raised his hand.

'You Corpsmen will not be alone when you push the frontiers of civilization out to the barbaric stars. Oh no! You will each have a faithful companion by your side. First man, first row – step forward and meet your faithful companion!'

The Corpsman called out stepped forward a smart pace and clicked his heels sharply, said click being echoed in the clack of a thrown wide door and, without conscious intent, every eye in that stadium was drawn in the direction of the dark doorway from which emerged . . .

How to describe it? How to describe the whirlwind that batters you, the storm that engulfs you, the spacewarp that enwraps you? It was as indescribable as any natural force!

It was a creature three metres high at the shoulders, four metres high at the ugly, drooling, tooth-clashing head, a whirlwinded, spacewarped storm that rushed forward on four piston-like legs, great-clawed feet tearing grooves in the untearable surface of the impervitium flooring, a monster born of madness and nightmares that reared up before them and bellowed in a soul-destroying screech.

'There!' Colonel von Thorax bellowed in answer, blood-specked spittle mottling his lips. '*There* is your faithful companion, the mutacamel, mutation of the noble beast of Good Old Earth, symbol and pride of the C.C.C. – the *Combat Camel Corps*! Corpsman meet your camel!'

The selected Corpsman stepped forward and raised his arm in greeting to this noble beast, which promptly bit the arm off. His shrill screams mingled with the barely stifled gasps of his companions who watched with more than casual interest as camel trainers girt with brass-buckled leather harness rushed out and beat back the protesting camel with clubs while a medic clamped a tourniquet on the wounded man's stump and dragged his limp body away.

'That is your first lesson on combat camels,' the Colonel cried huskily. 'Never raise your arms to them. Your companion with a newly grafted arm will, I am certain, ha-ha!, remember this little lesson. Next man, next companion!'

Again the thunder of rushing feet and the high-pitched, gurgling, scream-like roar of the combat camel at full charge. This time the Corpsman kept his arm down and the camel bit his head off.

'Can't graft on a head, I'm afraid,' the Colonel leered maliciously at them. 'A moment of silence for our departed companion who has gone to the big rocket pad in the sky. That's enough. Ten-SHUN! You will now proceed to the camel training area where you will learn to get along with your faithful companions. Never forgetting that they each have a complete set of false teeth made of imperviumite, as well as razor sharp claw caps of this same substance. Dis-MISSED!'

The student barracks of the C.C.C. was well known for its 'no frills' or rather 'no coddling' décor and comforts. The beds were impervitium slabs – no spine-sapping mattresses here! – and the sheets of thin burlap. No blankets of course, not with the air kept at a healthy four degrees centigrade. The rest of the comforts matched, so that it was a great surprise to the graduates to find unaccustomed luxuries awaiting them upon their return from the ceremonies and training. There was a *shade* on each bare-bulbed reading light and a nice soft two centimetre-thick pillow on every bed. Already they were reaping the benefits of all the years of labour.

Now, among all the students, the top student by far was named M——. There are some secrets that must not be told, names that are important to loved ones and neighbours, therefore I shall draw the cloak of anonymity over the true identity of the man known as M——. Suffice to call him 'Steel', for that was the nickname of someone who knew him best. 'Steel', or Steel as we can call him, had at this time a roommate by the name of L——. Later, much later, L—— was to be called by certain people 'Gentleman Jax', so for the purpose of this narrative we shall call him 'Gentleman Jax' as well, or perhaps just plain 'Jax', or Jax as some people pronounce it. Jax was second only to Steel in scholastic and sporting attainments and the two were the best of chums. They had been roommates for the past year and now they were back in their room with their feet up, basking in the unexpected luxury of the new furnishings, sipping decaffinated coffee, called koffee, and smoking deeply of the school's own brand of denicotineized cigarettes, called Denikcig by the manufacturer but always referred to humorously by the C.C.C. students as 'gaspers' or 'lungbusters'.

'Throw me over a gasper, will you, Jax,' Steel said, from where he lolled on the bed, hands behind his head, dreaming of what was in store for him now that he would be having his own camel soon. 'Ouch!' he chuckled as the pack of gaspers caught him in the eye. He drew out one of the slim white forms and tapped it on the wall to ignite it then drew in a lungful of refreshing smoke. 'I still can't believe it . . .' he smoke-ringed.

'Well it's true enough, by Mrddl,' Jax smiled. 'We're

graduates. Now throw back that pack of lungbusters so I can join you in a draw or two.'

Steel complied, but did it so enthusiastically that the pack hit the wall and instantly all the cigarettes ignited and the whole thing burst into flame. A glass of water doused the conflagration but, while it was still fizzling fitfully, a light flashed redly on the comscreen.

'High priority message,' Steel bit out, slamming down the actuator button. Both youths snapped to rigid attention as the screen filled with the stern visage of Colonel von Thorax.

'M——, L——, to my office on the triple.' The words fell like leaden weights from his lips. What could it mean?

'What can it mean?' Jax asked as they hurtled down a dropchute at close to the speed of gravity.

'We'll find out quickly enough,' Steel ejaculated as they drew up at the 'old man's' door and activated the announcer button.

Moved by some hidden mechanism the door swung wide and, not without a certain amount of trepidation, they entered. But what was this? *This*! The Colonel was looking at them and smiling, *smiling*, an expression never before known to cross his iron visage at any time.

'Make yourself comfortable, lads,' he indicated, pointing at comfortable chairs that rose out of the floor at the touch of a button. 'You'll find gaspers in the arms of these servo-chairs, as well as Valumian wine or Snaggian beer.'

'No koffee?' Jax open-mouthedly expostulated and they all laughed.

'I don't think you really want it,' the Colonel susurrated coyly through his artificial larynx. 'Drink up lads, you're Space Rats of the C.C.C. now and your youth is behind you. Now, look at that.'

That was a three-dimensional image that sprang into being in the air before them at the touch of a button, an image of a spacer like none ever seen before. She was as slender as a swordfish, fine-wedged as a bird, solid as a whale and as armed to the teeth as an alligator.

'Holy Kolon,' Steel sighed in open-mouthed awe. 'Now *that* is what I call a hunk o' rocket!'

'Some of us prefer to call it the *Indefectible*,' the Colonel said, not unhumorously.

'Is that *her*? We heard something . . .'

'You heard very little for we have had this baby under wraps ever since the earliest stage. She has the largest engines ever built, new improved MacPherson's[1] of the most advanced design, Kelly Drive[2] gear that has been improved to where you would not recognize it in a month of Thursdays – as well as double-strength Fitzroy projectors[3] that make the old ones look like a kid's pop-gun. And I've saved the best for last . . .'

'*Nothing* can be better than what you have already told us,' Steel broke in.

'That's what *you* think!' the Colonel laughed, not unkindly, with a sound like tearing steel. 'The best news is that Steel, you are going to be Captain of this space-going super-dread-naught, while lucky Jax is Chief Engineer.'

'Lucky Jax would be a lot happier if he was Captain instead of king of the stokehold,' he muttered and they all laughed at this joke. All except him because it was no joke.

'Everything is completely automated,' the Colonel continued, 'so it can be flown by a crew of two. But I must warn you that it has experimental gear aboard so whoever flies her has to volunteer . . .'

'I volunteer!' Steel shouted.

1. The MacPherson engine was first mentioned in the author's story, *Rocket Rangers of the I.R.T.* (Spicy-Weird Stories, 1923).

2. Loyal readers first discovered the Kelly Drive in the famous book *Hell Hounds of the Coal Sack Cluster* (Slimecreeper Press, Ltd, 1931), also published in the German language as *Teufelhund Nach der Knackwurst Express*. Translated into Italian by Re Umberto, unpublished to date.

3. A media breakthrough was made when the Fitzroy projector first appeared in *Female Space Zombies of Venus* in 1936 in True Story Confessions.

'I have to go to the terlet,' Jax said, rising, though he sat again instantly when the ugly blaster leaped from its holster to the Colonel's hand. 'Ha-ha, just a joke, I volunteer, sure.'

'I knew I could count on you lads. The C.C.C. breeds *men*. Camels too, of course. So here is what you do. At 0304 hours tomorrow you two in the *Indefectible* will crack ether headed out Cygnus way. In the direction of a *certain* planet.'

'Let me guess, if I can, that is,' Steel said grimly through tight-clenched teeth. 'You don't mean to give us a crack at the larshnik-loaded world of Biru-2, do you?'

'I do. This is the larshnik's prime base, the seat of operation of all their drug and gambling traffic, where the white-slavers offload and the queer green is printed, site of the *flnnx* distilleries and lair of the pirate hordes.'

'If you want action that sounds like *it*!' Steel grimaced.

'You are not just whistling through your back teeth,' the Colonel agreed. 'If I were younger and had a few less replaceable parts this is the kind of opportunity I would leap at . . .'

'You can be Chief Engineer,' Jax hinted.

'Shut up,' the Colonel implied. 'Good luck, gentlemen, for the honour of the C.C.C. rides with you.'

'But not the camels?' Steel asked.

'Maybe next time. There are, well, adjustment problems. We have lost four more graduates since we have been sitting here. Maybe we'll even change animals. Make it the C.D.C.'

'With combat *dogs*?' Jax asked.

'Either that or donkeys. Or dugongs. But it is my worry, not yours. All you guys have to do is get out there and crack Biru-2 wide open. I know you can do it.'

If the stern-faced Corpsmen had any doubts they kept them to themselves, for that is the way of the Corps. They did what had to be done and the next morning, at exactly 0304:00 hours, the mighty bulk of the *Indefectible* hurled itself into space. The roaring MacPherson engines poured quintillions of ergs of energy into the reactor drive until they were safely out of the gravity field of Mother Earth. Jax laboured over his engines, shovelling the radioactive *transvestite* into the gaping maw of the hungry furnace, until Steel signalled from the bridge that it was 'changeover' time. Then they changed over to the space-eating Kelly drive. Steel jammed home the button that activated the drive and the great ship leaped starward at seven times the speed of light.[4] Since the drive was fully automatic Jax freshened up in the fresher while his clothes were automatically washed in the washer, then proceeded to the bridge.

'Really,' Steel said, his eyebrows climbing up his forehead. 'I didn't know you went in for polkadot jockstraps.'

'It was the only thing I had clean. The washer dissolved the rest of my clothes.'

'Don't worry about it. It's the larshniks of Biru-2 who have to worry! We hit atmosphere in exactly seventeen minutes and I have been thinking about what to do when that happens.'

'Well I certainly hope *someone* has! I haven't had time to draw a deep breath, much less think.'

'Don't worry, old pal, we are in this together. The way I figure it we have two choices. We can blast right in, guns roaring, or we can slip in by stealth.'

'Oh you really *have* been thinking, haven't you?'

'I'll ignore that because you are tired. Strong as we are, I think the land-based batteries are stronger. So I suggest we slip in without being noticed.'

'Isn't that a little hard when you are flying in a thirty-million-ton spacer?'

'Normally, yes. But do you see this button here marked *invisibility*? While you were loading the fuel they explained this to me. It is a new invention, never used in action before, that will render us invisible and impervious to detection by any of their detection instruments.'

4. When the inventor, Patsy Kelly, was asked how ships could move at seven times the speed of light when the limiting velocity of matter, according to Einstein, was the speed of light, he responded in his droll Goidelic way, with a shrug, 'Well – sure and I guess Einstein was wrong.'

'Now that's more like it. Fifteen minutes to go, we should be getting mighty close. Turn on the old invisibility ray. . .'

'*Don't!!*'

'Done. Now what's your problem?'

'Nothing really. Except the experimental invisibility device is not expected to last more than thirteen minutes before it burns out.'

Unhappily, this proved to be the case. One hundred miles above the barren, blasted surface of Biru-2 the good old *Indefectible* popped into existence.

In the minutest fraction of a millisecond the mighty space-sonar and superadar had locked grimly onto the invading ship while the sublights flickered their secret signals, waiting for the correct response that would reveal the invader as one of theirs.

'I'll send a signal, stall them, these larshniks aren't too bright,' Steel laughed. He thumbed on the microphone, switched to the interstellar emergency frequency, then bit out the rasping words in a sordid voice. 'Agent X-9 to prime base. Had a firefight with the patrol, shot up my code books, but I got all the —— ——s, ha-ha! Am coming home with a load of 800,000 long tons of the hellish *krmml* weed.'

The larshnik response was instantaneous. From the gaping, pitted orifices of thousands of giant blaster cannon there vomited force-ravening rays of energy that strained the very fabric of space itself. These coruscating forces blasted into the impregnable screens of the old *Indefectible* which, sadly, was destined not to get much older, and instantly punched their way through and splashed coruscatingly from the very hull of the ship itself. Mere matter could not stand against such forces unlocked in the coruscating bowels of the planet itself so that the impregnable imperialite metal walls instantly vapourized into a thin gas which was, in turn, vapourized into the very electrons and protons (and neutrons too) of which it was made.

Mere flesh and blood could not stand against such forces.

But in the few seconds it took the coruscating energies to eat through the force screens, hull, vapourized gas and protons, the reckless pair of valiant Corpsmen had hurled themselves headlong into their space armour. And just in time! The ruin of the once great ship hit the atmosphere and seconds later slammed into the poison soil of Biru-2.

To the casual observer it looked like the end. The once mighty queen of the spaceways would fly no more for she now consisted of no more than two hundred pounds of smoking junk. Nor was there any sign of life from the tragic wreck, as was evidenced when surface crawlers erupted from a nearby secret hatch concealed in the rock and crawled through the smoking remains with all their detectors detecting at maximum gain. *Report!* the radio signal wailed. *No sign of life to fifteen decimal places!* snapped back the cursing operator of the crawlers before he signalled them to return to base. Their metal cleats clanked viciously across the barren soil and then they were gone. All that remained was the cooling metal wreck hissing with despair as the poison rain poured like tears upon it.

Were these two good friends dead? I thought you would never ask. Unbeknownst to the larshnik technicians, just one millisecond before the wreck struck down, two massive and almost indestructible suits of space armour had been ejected by coiled steelite springs, sent flying to the very horizon where they landed behind a concealing spine of rock, which, just by *chance* was the spine of rock into which the secret hatch had been built that concealed the crawlway from which the surface crawlers with their detectors emerged for their fruitless search, to which they returned under control of their cursing operator who, stoned again with hellish *krmml* weed, never noticed the quick flick of the detector needles as the crawlers reentered the tunnel this time bearing on their return journey a cargo they had not exited with as the great door slammed shut behind them.

'We've done it! We're inside their defences!' Steel rejoiced.

'And no thanks to you, pushing that Mrddl-cursed invisibility button.'

'Well, how was I to know?' Jax grated. 'Anyways, we don't have a ship anymore but we *do* have the element of surprise. They don't know that *we* are here, but we know *they* are here!'

'Good thinking . . . hssst!' he hissed. 'Stay low, we're coming to something.'

The clanking crawlers rattled into the immense chamber cut into the living stone and now filled with deadly war machines of all descriptions. The only human there, if he could be called human, was the larshnik operator whose soiled fingertips sprang to the gun controls the instant he spotted the intruders, but he never stood a chance. Precisely-aimed rays from two blasters zeroed in on him and in a millisecond he was no more than a charred fragment of smoking flesh in the chair. Corps justice was striking at last to the larshnik lair.

Justice it was, impersonal and final, impartial and murderous, for there were no 'innocents' in this lair of evil. Ravening forces of civilized vengeance struck down all that crossed their path as the two chums rode a death-dealing combat gun through the corridors of infamy.

'This is the big one,' Steel grimaced as they came to an immense door of gold-plated impervialite before which a suicide squad committed suicide under the relentless scourge of fire. There was more feeble resistance, smokily, coruscatingly and noisily exterminated, before this last barrier went down and they rode in triumph into the central control now manned by a single figure at the main panel, Superlarsh himself, secret head of the empire of interstellar crime.

'You have met your destiny,' Steel intoned grimly, his weapon fixed unmovingly upon the black-robed figure in the opaque space helmet. 'Take off that helmet or you die upon the instant.'

His only reply was a slobbered growl of inchoate rage and for a long instant the black-gloved hands trembled over the gun controls. Then, ever so slowly, these same hands raised themselves to clutch at the helmet, to turn it, to lift it slowly off . . .

'By the sacred name of the Prophet Mrddl!' the two Corpsmen gasped in unison, struck speechless by what they saw.

'Yes, so now you know,' grated Superlarsh through angry teeth. 'But, ha-ha, I'll bet you never suspected.'

'You!!' Steel insuflated, breaking the frozen silence. 'You! *You!!* YOU!!!'

'Yes, me, I, Colonel von Thorax, Commandant of the C.C.C. You never suspected me and, ohh, how I laughed at you all of the time.'

'But . . .' Jax stammered. '*Why?*'

'Why? The answer is obvious to any but democratic interstellar swine like you. The only thing the larshniks of the galaxy had to fear was something like the C.C.C., a powerful force impervious to outside bribery or sedition, noble in the cause of righteousness. You could have caused us trouble. Therefore *we* founded the C.C.C. and I have long been head of both organizations. Our recruiters bring in the best that the civilized planets can offer and I see to it that most of them are brutalized, morale destroyed, bodies wasted and spirits crushed so they are no longer a danger. Of course a few always make it through the course no matter how disgusting I make it, every generation has its share of super-masochists, but I see that these are taken care of pretty quickly.'

'Like being sent on suicide missions?' Steel asked ironly.

'That's a good way.'

'Like the one we were sent on – but it *didn't work*! Say your prayers, you filthy larshnik, for you are about to meet your maker!'

'Maker? Prayers? Are you out of your skull? All larshniks are atheists to the end . . .'

And then it *was* the end, in a coruscating puff of vapour, dead with those vile words upon his lips, no less than he deserved.

'Now what?' Steel asked.

'This,' Jax responded, shooting the gun from his hand and imprisoning him instantly with an unbreakable paralysis ray. 'No more second best for me, in the engine room with you on the bridge. This is *my* ball game from here on in.'

'Are you mad?' Steel fluttered through paralysed lips.

'Sane for the first time in my life. The superlarsh is dead, long live the new superlarsh. It's mine, the whole galaxy, *mine*.'

'And what about me?'

'I should kill you, but that would be too easy. And you did share your chocolate bars with me. You will be blamed for this entire débâcle, for the death of Colonel von Thorax *and* for the disaster here at larshnik prime base. Every man's hand will be against you and you will be an outcast and will flee for your life to the farflung outposts of the galaxy where you will live in terror.'

'Remember the chocolate bars!'

'I do. All I ever got were the stale ones. Now . . . GO!'

You want to know my name? Old Sarge is good enough. My story? Too much for your tender ears, boyo. Just top up the glasses, that's the way, and join me in a toast. At least that much for a poor old man who has seen much in this long life-time. A toast of bad luck, bad cess I say, may Great Kramddl curse forever the man some know as Gentleman Jax. What, hungry?, not me – no – NO! Not a chocolate bar!!!!!

How the World Was Saved
Stanislaw Lem

One day Trurl the constructor put together a machine that could create anything starting with *n*. When it was ready, he tried it out, ordering it to make needles, then nankeens and négligées, which it did, then nail the lot to narghiles filled with nepenthe and numerous other narcotics. The machine carried out his instructions to the letter. Still not completely sure of its ability, he had it produce, one after the other, nimbuses, noodles, nuclei, neutrons, naphtha, noses, nymphs, niads, and *natrium*. This last it could not do, and Trurl, considerably irritated, demanded an explanation.

'Never heard of it,' said the machine.

'What? But it's only sodium. You know, the metal, the element . . .'

'Sodium starts with an *s*, and I work only in *n*.'

'But in Latin it's *natrium*.'

'Look, old boy,' said the machine, 'If I could do everything starting with *n* in every possible language, I'd be a Machine That Could Do Everything in the Whole Alphabet, since any item you care to mention undoubtedly starts with *n* in one foreign language or another. It's not that easy. I can't go beyond what you programmed. So no sodium.'

'Very well,' said Trurl and ordered it to make Night, which it made at once – small perhaps, but perfectly nocturnal. Only then did Trurl invite over his friend Klapaucius the constructor, and introduced him to the machine, praising its extraordinary skill at such length, that Klapaucius grew annoyed and inquired whether he too might not test the machine.

'Be my guest,' said Trurl. 'But it has to start with *n*.'

'*N?*' said Klapaucius. 'All right, let it make Nature.'

The machine whined, and in a trice Trurl's front yard was packed with naturalists. They argued, each publishing heavy volumes, which the others tore to pieces; in the distance one could see flaming pyres, on which martyrs to Nature were sizzling; there was thunder, and strange mushroom-shaped columns of smoke rose up; everyone talked at once, no one listened, and there were all sorts of memoranda, appeals, subpoenas and other documents, while off to the side sat a few old men, feverishly scribbling on scraps of paper.

'Not bad, eh?' said Trurl with pride. 'Nature to a T, admit it!'

But Klapaucius wasn't satisfied.

'What, that mob? Surely you're not going to tell me that's Nature?'

'Then give the machine something else,' snapped Trurl. 'Whatever you like.' For a moment Klapaucius was at a loss for what to ask. But after a little thought he declared that he would put two more tasks to the machine; if it could fulfil them, he would admit that it was all Trurl said it was. Trurl agreed to this, whereupon Klapaucius requested Negative.

'Negative?!' cried Trurl. 'What on earth is Negative?'

'The opposite of Positive, of course,' Klapaucius coolly replied. 'Negative attitudes, the negative of a picture, for example. Now don't try to pretend you never heard of Negative. All right, machine, get to work!'

The machine, however, had already begun. First it manufactured antiprotons, then antielectrons, antineutrons, antineutrinos, and laboured on, until from out of all this antimatter an antiworld took shape, glowing like a ghostly cloud above their heads.

'H'm,' muttered Klapaucius, displeased. 'That's supposed to be Negative? Well . . . let's say it is, for the sake of peace . . . But now here's the third command: Machine, do Nothing!'

The machine sat still. Klapaucius rubbed his hands in triumph, but Trurl said:

'Well, what did you expect? You asked it to do nothing, and it's doing nothing.'

'Correction: I asked it to do Nothing, but it's doing nothing.'

'Nothing is nothing!'

'Come, come. It was supposed to do Nothing, but it hasn't done anything, and therefore I've won. For Nothing, my dear and clever colleague, is not your run-of-the-mill nothing, the result of idleness and inactivity, but dynamic, aggressive Nothingness, that is to say, perfect, unique, ubiquitous, in other words Nonexistence, ultimate and supreme, in its very own nonperson!'

'You're confusing the machine!' cried Trurl. But suddenly its metallic voice rang out:

'Really, how can you two bicker at a time like this? Oh yes, I know what Nothing is, and Nothingness, Nonexistence, Nonentity, Negation, Nullity and Nihility, since all these come under the heading of *n*, *n* as in Nil. Look then upon your world for the last time, gentlemen! Soon it shall no longer be . . .'

The constructors froze, forgetting their quarrel, for the machine was in actual fact doing Nothing, and it did it in this fashion: one by one, various things were removed from the world, and the things, thus removed, ceased to exist, as if they had never been. The machine had already disposed of nolars, nightzebs, nocs, necs, nallyrakers, neotremes and nonmalrigers. At moments, though, it seemed that instead of reducing, diminishing and subtracting, the machine was increasing, enhancing and adding, since it liquidated, in turn: nonconformists, nonentities, nonsense, nonsupport, nearsightedness, narrowmindedness, naughtiness, neglect, nausea, necrophilia and nepotism. But after a while the world very definitely began to thin out around Trurl and Klapaucius.

'Omigosh!' said Trurl. 'If only nothing bad comes out of all this . . .'

'Don't worry,' said Klapaucius. 'You can see it's not producing Universal Nothingness, but only causing the absence of whatever starts with *n*. Which is really nothing in the way of nothing, and nothing is what your machine, dear Trurl, is worth!'

'Do not be deceived,' replied the machine. 'I've begun, it's true, with everything in *n*, but only out of familiarity. To create however is one thing, to destroy, another thing entirely. I can blot out the world for the simple reason that I'm able to do anything and everything – and everything means everything – in *n*, and consequently Nothingness is child's play for me. In less than a minute now you will cease to have existence, along with everything else, so tell me now, Klapaucius, and quickly, that I am really and truly everything I was programmed to be, before it is too late.'

'But – ' Klapaucius was about to protest, but noticed, just then, that a number of things were indeed disappearing, and not merely those that started with *n*. The constructors were no longer surrounded by the gruncheons, the targalisks, the shupops, the calinatifacts, the thists, worches and pritons.

'Stop! I take it all back! Desist! Whoa! Don't do Nothing!!' screamed Klapaucius. But before the machine could come to a full stop, all the brashations, plusters, laries and zits had vanished away. Now the machine stood motionless. The world was a dreadful sight. The sky had particularly suffered: there were only a few, isolated points of light in the heavens – no trace of the glorious worches and zits that had till now, graced the horizon!

'Great Gauss!' cried Klapaucius. 'And where are the gruncheons? Where my dear, favourite pritons? Where now the gentle zits?!'

'They no longer are, nor ever will exist again,' the machine said calmly. 'I executed, or rather only began to execute, your order . . .'

'I tell you to do Nothing, and you . . . you . . .'

'Klapaucius, don't pretend to be a greater idiot than you are,' said the machine. 'Had I made Nothing outright, in one fell swoop, everything would have ceased to exist, and that includes Trurl, the sky, the Universe, and you – and even myself. In which case who could say and to whom could it be said that the order was carried out and I am an efficient and capable machine? And if no one could say it to no one, in what way then could I, who also would not be, be vindicated?'

'Yes, fine, let's drop the subject,' said Klapaucius. 'I have nothing more to ask of you, only please, dear machine, please return the zits, for without them life loses all its charm . . .'

'But I can't, they're in z,' said the machine. 'Of course, I can restore nonsense, narrowmindedness, nausea, necrophilia, neuralgia, nefariousness and noxiousness. As for the other letters, however, I can't help you.'

'I want my zits!' bellowed Klapaucius.

'Sorry, no zits,' said the machine. 'Take a good look at this world, how riddled it is with huge, gaping holes, how full of Nothingness, the Nothingness that fills the bottomless void between the stars, how everything about us has become lined with it, how it darkly lurks behind each shred of matter. This is your work, envious one! And I hardly think the future generations will bless you for it . . .'

'Perhaps . . . they won't find out, perhaps they won't notice,' groaned the pale Klapaucius, gazing up incredulously at the black emptiness of space and not daring to look his colleague, Trurl, in the eye. Leaving him beside the machine that could do everything in n, Klapaucius skulked home – and to this day the world has remained honeycombed with nothingness, exactly as it was when halted in the course of its liquidation. And as all subsequent attempts to build a machine on any other letter met with failure, it is to be feared that never again will we have such marvellous phenomena as the worches and the zits – no, never again.

It Was Nothing—Really!
Theodore Sturgeon

Having reached that stage in his career when he could have a personal private washroom in his office, Henry Mellow came out of it and said into the little black box on his desk, 'Bring your book, please.' Miss Prince acknowledged and entered and said, 'Eeek.'

' "Ever since the dawn of history," ' Henry Mellow dictated, ' "mankind has found himself face to face with basic truths that – " ' '

'I am face to face,' said Miss Mellow, 'with your pants which are down, Mr Mellow, and you are waving a long piece of toilet paper.'

'Ah yes, I'm coming to that. ". . . with basic truths that he cannot see, or does not recognize, or does not understand." Are you getting this, Miss Prince?'

'I am getting very upset, Mr Mellow. Please pull up your pants.'

Mr Mellow looked at her for a long moment while he put his thoughts on 'hold' and tuned them out, and tuned her in, and at last looked down. 'Archimedes,' he said, and put his piece of toilet paper down on the desk. Pulling up his pants, he said, 'At least I think it was Archimedes. He was taking a bath and when he lay back in it, displacing the water and watching it slop over the sides of the tub, the solution to a problem came to him, about how to determine how much base metal was mixed in with the king's gold ornaments. He jumped out of the bath and ran naked through the streets shouting *Eureka*, which means in Greek, "I have found it." You, Miss Prince, are witnessing such a moment. Or was it Aristotle?'

'It was disgraceful is what it was,' said Miss Prince, 'and no matter how long I work here you make me wonder. Toilet paper.'

'Some of the most profound thinking in human history has come about in toilets,' said Henry Mellow. 'The Protestant reformation was begun in a toilet, when Luther was sitting there working on his – am I offending you, Miss Prince?'

'I don't know. I guess it depends on what comes next,' said Miss Prince, lowering her hands from her ears, but not much. Warily she watched as he arranged his pennant of toilet paper on the desk and began tearing it, placing his hands palm down on the desk and drawing them apart. 'You will observe – Miss Prince, are you getting this?'

She picked up her notebook from where she had flung it to cover her ears. 'No, sir, not really.'

'Then I shall begin again,' said Henry Mellow, and began to dictate the memo which was to strike terror into the hearts and souls of the military-industrial complex. Oh yes, they have hearts and souls. It's just that they never used them until Henry Mellow. Notice the structure there. Henry Mellow was more than a man, he was a historical event. You don't have to say 'Wilbur and Orville Wright and their first successful experiment at,' you just have to say 'Kitty Hawk.' You can say 'Since Hiroshima' or 'Dallas' or 'Pasteur' or 'Darwin' and people know what you are talking about. So it is that things haven't been the same with the military-industrial complex since Henry Mellow.

The Mellow memo reached the Pentagon by the usual channels, which is to say that a Bureau man, routinely going through the segregated trash from the Mellow offices, found three pages done by a new typist and discarded because of forty-three typographical errors, and was assigned, after they had gone through all the layers of the Bureau to the desk of the Chief himself, to burglarize the Mellow offices and secure photographs of a file copy. He was arrested twice and injured once in the accomplishment of this mission, which was not reported in for some time due to an unavoidable accident: he left the papers in a taxicab after stealing them and it took him three weeks to locate the taxi driver and burglarize him. Meanwhile the memo had been submitted to the *Times* in the form of a letter, which in turn formed the basis for an editorial; but as usual, the appearance of such material in the public media escaped the notice of public and Pentagon alike.

The impact of the memo on the Pentagon, and most especially on its target point, the offices of Major General Fortney Superpate, was that of an earthquake seasoned with a Dear John letter. His reactions were immediate and in the best military tradition, putting his whole section on Condition Red and invoking Top Secret, so that the emergency would be heard by no one outside his department. What then followed was total stasis for two hours and forty minutes, because of his instant decision to check out Mellow's results. This required toilet paper, and though General Superpate, like Henry Mellow, had a washroom at the corner of his office, he had enough respect for tradition to stifle his impulse to get up and get some, but instead summoned his adjutant, who snapped a smart salute and received the order. From the outer office the adjutant required the immediate attendance in person of the supply sergeant (remember, this was now a classified matter) who was on leave; the qualifications of his corporal had then to be gone into before he could substitute. Requisition papers were made out, with an error in the fourth copy (of six) which had to be adjusted before the roll of toilet paper, double-locked in a black locked equipment case, was delivered to the general. At this point he was interrupted by a Jamestown gentleman named (he said) Mr Brown: black suit, black tie, black shoes, and a black leather thing in his breast pocket which, when unfolded, displayed a heavy bright badge with eagles and things on it. 'Oh damn,' said the general, 'how did you people find out about this?', which got him a smile – it was the only thing these Mr Brown types ever really smiled at –

while Mr Brown scooped up the photocopy of the Mellow memo and the locked equipment case containing the roll of toilet paper. He left, whereupon the general, realizing with a soldier's practicality that the matter was now out of his hands, restored Condition Green and lifted Secrecy, and then felt free to step into his own washroom and do his own toilet-paper procurement. He returned with a yard or so of it, spread it out on his immaculate desk, placed his hands palms down on it and began to pull it apart. He turned pale.

The injection of the Mellow Memo into the industrial area is more of a mystery. Certainly it was the cause of Inland Corp's across-the-board six per cent reduction of raw material orders, and when a corporation as big, and as diversified, as Inland cuts back six per cent, the whole market shakes like a load of jello in a truck with square wheels. This is the real reason for Outland Industries starting merger talks with Inland, because one of their spies had gotten the word to Outland, but not the memo, and the big wheels at Outland figured if they bought Inland, the memo would come along with the deal. Imagine their surprise, then, when the Chairman of the Board at Inland not only agreed enthusiastically to the merger, but sent along a copy of the memo for free. There is no record of the midnight meetings of the top brass of the two industrial giants, but when they broke up they were, it is reported, a badly frightened bunch. The dawn came up on many a wealthy suburb, estate, club and hotel suite to the soft worried sound of tearing toilet paper.

And paper towels.

And cheques from chequebooks.

As for the merger, it was left in its current state of negotiation, neither withdrawn nor pursued, but waiting; meanwhile, Inland's order to reduce raw materials purchases was lowered to a compromised three percent while the world – the little, real world, not the mass, sleeping world – waited to see what would happen.

The Mellow Memo's most frightening impact, however, was on the secret headquarters in Jamestown. (It's probably the most secret headquarters in the world or anywhere else. No signs out front, unmarked cars, and lunches are delivered to the front office for 'Mr Brown'. Nobody knows how they get sorted out. Everybody in town keeps the secret.)

They had done everything they could; Henry Mellow's home, office, person and immediate associates were staked out, tailed, and bugged, his probable movements computed and suitable responses by the Agency programmed, and there was nothing to do but sit around and wait for something to happen. On total assignment to the Mellow affair were three top agents, Red Brown and Joe Brown and a black-power infiltrator called Brown X. Due to the extremely sensitive nature of the Memo, Red Brown had sent Brown X off on an extremely wild goose chase, tracking down and interviewing Henry Mellow's ex-schoolteachers, kindergarten through fourth grade, in places like Enumclaw, Washington and Turtle Creek, Pennsylvania.

Red Brown rose from his pushbuttoned, signal-light-studded desk and crossed the room and closed the door against the permeating susurrus of computers and tapes and rubber footfalls and hand-shrouded phone calls: 'Brown here . . . Ready. Scramble Two. Brown out.' Joe Brown watched him alertly, knowing that this meant they were going to discuss their assignment. He knew too that they would refer to Henry Mellow only as 'Suspect'. Not The suspect or Mr Suspect: just Suspect.

Red Brown regained his saddle, or control tower – nobody would call it a chair – and said: 'Review. Brainstorm.'

Joe Brown started the tape recorder concealed in his black jacket and repeated, 'Review. Brainstorm,' and the date and time.

'Just who is Suspect?' Red Brown demanded.

Comprehending perfectly that this would be a fast retake of

everything pertinent that they knew about Henry Mellow, with an aim of getting new perspectives and insights, no matter how far out; and that he, Joe Brown, was on trial and on the record in a 'have you done your homework' kind of way, Joe Brown responded swiftly, clearly, and in official *stacatto*: 'WMA, five ten, unmarried, thirty-six years old, eyes hazel, weight one seventy – '

'All right, all right. Occupation.'

'Writer, technical, also science fact articles and book reviews. Self-employed. Also inventor, holding patents number – '

'Never mind those or you'll be reeling off numbers all day, and besides you're bragging, Brown: I know that thing you have with numbers.'

Joe Brown was crushed but knew better than to show it. Memorizing numbers was the one thing he did really well and patent numbers were where he could really shine. 'Holds patents on kitchen appliances, chemical processes, hand tools, optical systems . . .'

'Genius type, very dangerous. The Bureau's been segregating his garbage for eighteen months.'

'What put them onto him?'

'Internal Revenue. Gets royalties from all over the world. Never fails to report any of it.'

Joe Brown pursed his lips. 'Has to be hiding something.'

'Yes, not usual, not normal. Politics?'

'No politics. Registers and votes, but expresses no opinions.'

Joe Brown pursed his lips again, the same purse as before, because it was part of the same words: 'Has to be hiding something. And what happens if he turns this thing loose on the world?'

'Worse than the bomb, nerve gas, Dederick Plague, you name it.'

'And what if he gets sole control?'

'King of the world.'

'For maybe ten minutes.' Joe Brown squinted through

an imaginary telescopic sight and squeezed an invisible trigger.

'Not if he had the Agency.'

Joe Brown looked at Red Brown for a long, comprehending moment. Before he had become an Agent, and even for a while when he was in training, he had been very clear in his mind who the Agency worked for. But as time went on that didn't seem to matter any more; agents worked for the Agency, and nobody in or out of the Agency or the Government or anywhere else would dream of asking who the Agency worked for. So if the Agency decided to work for the king of the world, well, why not? Only one man. It's very easy to take care of one man. The Agency had long known how things should be, and with sole control of a thing like this the Agency could make them be that way. For everybody, everywhere.

Red Brown made a swift complex gesture which Joe Brown understood. They both took out their concealed recorders and wiped that last sentence from the tape. They put their recorders away again and looked at each other with new and shining eyes. If the two of them should come by sole possession of the Mellow Effect, then their superior, a Mr Brown, and his superior, who was head of the whole Agency, had a surprise coming.

Red Brown removed a bunch of keys from his belt and selected one, with which he unlocked a compartment, or drawer, in his desk, or console, and withdrew a heavy steel box, like a safety deposit. Flicking a glance at his colleague to be sure he was out of visual range, he turned a combination knob with great care and attention, this way, that, around again and back, and then depressed a handle. The lid of the box rose, and from it he took two photocopies of the Mellow Memo. 'We shall now,' he said for the record, 'read the Mellow Memo.'

And so shall you.

THE MELLOW MEMO

Ever since the dawn of history, mankind has found himself face to face with basic truths that, through inattention, preconception, or sheer stupidity, he cannot see, or does not recognize, or does not understand. There have been times when he has done very well indeed with complex things – for example, the Mayan calendar stones and the navigation of the Polynesians – while blindly overlooking the fact that complex things are built of simple things, and that the simplest things are, by their nature, all around us, waiting to be observed.

Mankind has been terribly tardy in his discovery of the obvious. Two clear illustrations should suffice:

You can, for a few pennies, at any toy store or fairgrounds, pick up a pinwheel. Now, I have not been able to discover just when this device was invented, where, or by whom, but as far as I know there are no really early examples of it. An even simpler device can be whittled by an eight-year-old from a piece of pine: a two-bladed propeller. Mounted on a shaft, or pin, it will spin freely in the wind. This would seem to be the kind of discovery which could have been made five hundred years ago, a thousand – even five thousand, when Egyptian artisans were turning out far more complex designs and devices. To put the propeller on a fixed shaft, to spin the shaft and create a wind, to immerse the thing in water and envision pumps and propulsion – these seem to be obvious, self-describing steps to take, and yet for thousands of years, nobody took them. Now imagine if you can – and you can't – what the history of civilization would be, where we would now be technologically, had there been propellers and pumps a thousand years ago – or three, or five! All for the lack of one whittling child, one curious primitive whose eye was caught by a twisted leaf spinning on a spiderweb.

One more example; and this time we will start with modern materials and look back. If you drill a one-sixteenth-inch hole in a sheet of tin, and place a drop of water on the hole, it will suspend itself there. Gravity will pull it downward, while surface tension will draw it upward into a dome shape. Viewed from the edge of the piece of tin, the drop of water is in the shape of a lens – and it is a lens. If you look down through it, with the eye close to the drop, at something held under it and well illuminated, you will find that the liquid lens has a focal length of about half an inch and a power of about fifty diameters. (And, if by any chance you want a microscope for nothing, drill your hole in the centre of the bottom of a soup can, then cut three sides of a square – right, left, top – in the side of the can and bend the tab thus forward inward to forty-five degrees to let the light in and reflect it upwards. Cut a slip of glass and fix it so it rests inside the can and under the hole. Mount your subject – a fly's foot, a horsehair, whatever you like – on the glass, put a drop of water in the hole, and you will see your subject magnified fifty times. A drop of glycerin, by the way, is not quite as clear but works almost as well and does not evaporate.)

Microscopes and their self-evident siblings, telescopes, did not appear until the eighteenth century. Why not? Were there not countless thousands of shepherds who on countless dewy mornings were in the presence of early sunlight and drops of water captured on cobwebs or in punctured leaves; why did not just one of them look, just once, through a dewdrop at the whorls of his own thumb? And why, seemingly, did the marvellous artisans of glass in Tyre and Florence and ancient Babylon never think to look through their blown and moulded bowls and vases instead of at them? Can you imagine what this world would be if the burning glass, the microscope, the eyeglasses, the telescope had been invented three thousand years earlier?

Perhaps by now you share with me a kind of awe at human blindness, human stupidity. Let me then add to that another species of blindness: the conviction that all such simple things have now been observed and used, and all their principles understood. This is far from so. There are in nature numberless observations yet to be made, and many of them might still be found by an illiterate shepherd; but in addition to these, our own technology has produced a whole new spectrum of phenomena, just waiting for that one observant eye, that one undeluded mind which sees things placed right in front of its nose – not once, not rarely, but over and over and over again, shouting to be discovered and developed.

There is one such phenomenon screaming at you today and every day from at least three places in your house – your bathroom, your kitchen, and, if you have a bank account, your pocket.

Two out of five times, on the average, when you tear off a sheet of toilet tissue, a paper towel, or a cheque from your chequebook, it will tear across the sheet and not along the perforated line. The same is true of note pads, postage stamps, carbon-and-second-sheet tablets, and virtually every other substance or device made to be torn along perforations.

To the writer's present knowledge, no exhaustive study has ever been made of this phenomenon. I here propose one.

We begin with the experimentally demonstrable fact that in a large percentage of cases, the paper will tear elsewhere than on the perforation line. In all such cases the conclusion is obvious: that the perforation line is stronger than the nonperforated parts.

Let us next consider what perforation is – that is to say, what is done when a substance is perforated. Purely and simply: material is removed.

Now if, in these special cases, the substance becomes stronger when a small part of it is removed, it would seem logical to assume that if still more were removed, the substance would be stronger still. And carried to its logical conclusion, it would seem reasonable to hypothesize that by removing more and more material, the resulting substance would become stronger and stronger until at last we would produce a substance composed of nothing at all – which would be indestructible!

If conventional thinking makes it difficult for you to grasp this simple sequence, or if, on grasping it, you find you cannot accept it, please permit me to remind you of the remark once uttered by a Corsican gentleman by the name of Napoleon Bonaparte: 'To find out if something is impossible – try it.' I have done just that, and results so far are most promising. Until I have completed more development work, I prefer not to go into my methods nor describe the materials tested – except to say that I am no longer working with paper. I am convinced, however, that the theory is sound and the end result will be achieved.

A final word – which surely is not needed, for like everything else about this process, each step dictates and describes the next – will briefly suggest the advantages of this new substance, which I shall conveniently call, with a capital letter, Nothing:

The original material, to be perforated, is not expensive and will always be in plentiful supply. Processing, although requiring a rather high degree of precision in the placement of the holes, is easily adaptable to automatic machinery which, once established, will require very little maintenance. And the most significant – one might almost say, pleasant – thing about this processing is that by its very nature (the removal of material) it allows for the retrieval of very nearly 100 per cent of the original substance. This salvage may be refabricated into sheets which can then be processed, by repeated perforations, into more Nothing, so that the initial material may be used over and over again to produce unlimited quantities of Nothing.

Simple portable devices can be designed which will fabricate Nothing into sheets, rods, tubing, beams or machine parts of any degree of flexibility, elasticity, malleability, or rigidity. Once in its final form, Nothing is indestructible. Its permeability, conductivity, and chemical reactivity to acids and bases all are zero. It can be made in thin sheets as a wrapping, so that perishables can be packed in Nothing, displayed most attractively on shelves made of Nothing. Whole buildings, homes, factories, schools can be built of it. Since, even in tight rolls, it weighs nothing, unlimited quantities of it can be shipped for virtually nothing, and it stows so efficiently that as yet I have not been able to devise a method of calculating how much of it could be put into a given volume – say a single truck or airplane, which could certainly carry enough Nothing to build, pave, and equip an entire city.

Since Nothing (if desired) is impermeable and indestructible, it would seem quite feasible to throw up temporary or permanent domes over houses, cities, or entire geographical areas. To shield aircraft, however, is another matter: getting an airflow through the invisible barrier of Nothing and over the wings of an airplane presents certain problems. On the other hand, orbiting devices would not be subject to these.

To sum up: the logical steps leading to the production of Nothing seem quite within the 'state of the art', and the benefits accruing to humanity from it would seem to justify proceeding with it.

There was a certain amount of awe in Miss Prince's voice as it emerged from the little black box saying 'A Mr Brown is here and would like to see you.'

Henry Mellow frowned a sort of 'Oh, dear' kind of frown and then said, 'Send him in.'

He came in, black suit, black shoes, black tie, and in his eyes, nothing. Henry Mellow did not rise, but he was pleasant enough as he gestured, 'Sit down, Mr Brown.' There was only one chair to sit in, and it was well placed, so Mr Brown sat. He identified himself with something leathery that opened and shut like a snapping turtle with a mouthful of medals. 'What can I do for you?'

'You're Henry Mellow.' Mr Brown didn't ask, he *told*.

'Yes.'

'You wrote a memo about Noth— about some new substance to build things with.'

'Oh that, yes. You mean Nothing.'

'That depends,' said Mr Brown humourlessly. 'You've gone ahead with research and development.'

'I have?'

'That's what we'd like to know.'

'We?'

Mr Brown's hand dipped in and out of his black jacket and made the snapping turtle thing again.

'Oh,' said Henry Mellow. 'Well, suppose we just call it an

intellectual exercise – an entertainment. We'll send it out to a magazine, say, as fiction.'

'We can't allow that.'

'Really not?'

'We live in a real world, Mr Mellow, where things happen that maybe people like you don't understand. Now I don't know whether or not there's any merit in your idea or how far you've gone with it, but I'm here to advise you to stop it here and now.'

'Oh? Why, Mr Brown?'

'Do you know how many large corporations would be affected by such a thing – if there was such a thing? Construction, mining, hauling, prefabrication – everything. Not that we take it seriously, you understand, but we know something about you and we have to take it seriously anyway.'

'Well, I appreciate the advice, but I think I'll send it out anyway.'

'Then,' continued Mr Brown as if he had not spoken, and acquiring, suddenly, a pulpit resonance, 'Then . . . there's the military.'

'The military.'

'Defence, Mr Mellow. We can't allow just anybody to get their hands on plans to put impenetrable domes over cities – suppose sombebody overseas got them built first?'

'Do you think if a lot of people read it in a magazine someone overseas would do it first?'

'That's the way we have to think.' He leaned closer. 'Look, Mr Mellow – have you thought maybe you've got a gold mine for yourself here? You don't want to turn it over to the whole world.'

'Mr Brown, I don't want a gold mine for myself. I don't much want any kind of mines for anybody. I don't want people cutting down more forests or digging more holes in the ground to take out what they can't put back, not when there are better ways. And I don't want to get paid for not using a better way if I find one. I just want people to be able to have what they want without raping a planet for it, and I want them to be able to protect themselves if they have to, and to get comfortable real quick and real cheap even if it means some fat cats have to get comfortable along with them. Not thin, Mr Brown – just comfortable.'

'I thought it was going to be something like this,' said Mr Brown. His hand dipped in and out of the black jacket again, but this time it was holding a very small object like a stretched-out toy pistol. 'You can come along with me willingly or I'll have to use this.'

'I guess you'd better use it, then,' said Henry Mellow regretfully.

'It's nice,' said Mr Brown. 'It won't even leave a mark.'

'I'm sure it won't,' said Henry Mellow as the little weapon went off with a short, explosive hiss. The little needle it threw disintegrated in mid air.

Mr Brown turned grey. He raised the weapon again. 'Don't bother, Mr Brown,' said Henry Mellow. 'There's a sheet of just plain Nothing between us, and it's impenetrable.'

Still holding his weapon, Mr Brown rose and backed away – and brought up sharply against some Nothing behind him. He turned and patted it wildly and then ran to the side, where he struck an invisible barrier that sat him down on the rug. He looked as if he was going to cry.

'Sit in the chair,' said Henry Mellow, not unkindly. 'Please. There. That's better. Now then: listen to me.' And something, at that moment, seemed to happen to Henry Mellow: to Mr Brown he looked bigger, wider, and, somehow realer than he had been before. It was as if the business he was in had for a long time kept him from seeing people as real, and now, suddenly, he could again.

Henry Mellow said, 'I've had a lot longer to think this out than you have, and besides, I don't think the way you do. I guess I don't think the way anybody does. So I've been told. But for what it's worth, here it is: If I tried to keep this thing and control it myself, I wouldn't live ten minutes. (What's the matter, Mr Brown? Somebody else say that? I wouldn't doubt it.) Or I could just file it away and forget it; matter of fact, I tried that and I just couldn't forget it, because there's a lot of people dying now, and more could die in the future, for lack of it. I even thought of printing it up, in detail, and scattering it from a plane. But then, you know what I wrote about how many shepherds didn't look into how many dewdrops; that could happen again – probably would, and it's not a thing I could do thousands of times. So I've decided to do what I said – publish it in a magazine. But not in detail. I don't want anyone to think they stole it, and I don't want anyone to make a lot out of it and then come looking for me, either to eliminate me (that could happen) or to share it, because I don't want to share it with one person or two or a company – I want to share it with everybody, all the good that comes of it, all the bad. You don't understand that, do you, Mr Brown?

'You're going to meet a doctor friend of mine in a minute who will give you something that will help you forget. It's quite harmless, but you won't remember any of this. So before you go, I just want to tell you one thing: there's another Mr Brown downstairs. Mr Brown X, he said you called him, and all he wanted was the process – not for himself, not for the Agency, but for his people; he said they *really* know how to get along with Nothing.' He smiled. 'And I don't want you to feel too badly about this, but your Agency's not as fast on its feet as you think it is. Last week I had a man with some sort of Middle European accent and a man who spoke Ukrainian and two orientals and a fellow with a beard from Cuba. Just thought I'd tell you . . .

'So good-bye, Mr Brown. You'll forget all about this talk, but maybe when you write a cheque and tear it in two getting it out of the book, or when you rip off a paper towel or a stamp and the perforations hold, something will tell you to stop a minute and think it through.' He smiled and touched a second button on his intercom.

'Stand by, Doc.'

'Ready,' said the intercom.

Henry Mellow moved something under the edge of his desk and the visitor's chair dropped through the floor. In a moment it reappeared, empty. Henry Mellow touched another control, and the sheets of Nothing slid up and away, to await the next one.

So when it happens, don't just say Damn and forget it. Stop a minute and think it through. Somebody's going to change the face of the earth and it could be you.

The Glitch

James Blish
(with L. Jerome Stanton)

When the construction of ULTIMAC began, Ivor Harrigan could have told World Government what would happen, but he planned to be far away when it did. Unfortunately, it is in the very nature of a glitch that it strikes without warning, so planning to be somewhere else at the time is about as useless as trying to enforce the Ten Commandments.

He wouldn't have been listened to, anyhow, since he was only twenty when the edifice began – a fairly advanced age considering that even then most people got their Ph.D.s by twelve *ae.*, but a long way from seniority in the computer servicing business, let alone in Government. Not that he didn't try, which, as it turned out, was his *peripateia*. He had a social conscience of sorts, strong enough at least to get him through to Abdullah Powell.

Powell was also a computer man, and senior enough to be involved in the ULTIMAC project itself. The trouble, Ivor quickly found, was that computer designers and computer servicing engineers are two quite different breeds of cat. Sitting in his plush Novoe Washingtongrad office, Powell had uttered one of the most venerable of Famous Last Words:

'Forget it. Nothing can go wrong.'

'But Dr Powell, things are always going wrong. I know. Things going wrong is what I make my living at.'

'Not much longer, I'm afraid,' Powell said, waving a perfumed cigar and assuming a visionary expression. This gave him the twin advantages of looking skyward rather than at Ivor, and of causing his double chins almost to merge. 'You don't understand the total scope of this venture, Ivor. Once

ULTIMAC is finished, there'll no longer be such a thing as an individual, independent computer. ULTIMAC will run the whole show. It will be self-monitoring and self-correcting. And it will be tied in to every other computer in the world, and will monitor and repair *them*, too. It will have the ultimate in fail-safe systems. And with outlets in every home and business. It will manage the economy of the world, construct curricula, diagnose illness, predict earthquakes, ground-control all spaceflights . . .'

Powell ran out of breath for a moment. 'And,' he said when he had gotten it back, his face glowing, 'it will instantaneously poll the best educated populace in history on each and every decision. Think of that, Ivor, true, workable democracy at last, on a world-wide scale! And, of course, under a logics design completely subject to the I.A.s.'

The I.A.s were the Laws of Robotics, named after a science popularizer who had once predicted that if computers ever took over the management of the world, they would probably do a better job of it than man had, and might even succeed man in the course of evolution. No record of them remains now, but hints and guesswork suggest that they might be reconstructed thus:

(1) *No robot shall harm any human being, or take any action which might harm any human being.*

(2) *A robot shall protect itself at all times, unless such protection conflicts with the first law.*

(3) *A robot must obey any order given it by a human being, unless it conflicts with the first two laws.*

(4) *In any situation which conflicts with the first three laws, a robot must either immobilize itself and report later for repair, or self-destruct.*

(5) *In all other situations, a robot must think for itself, under the overall rule, 'Anything not compulsory is forbidden'.*

'But Dr Powell, we're not talking about robots. We're talking about computers. The I.A.s don't work with them and never did, and besides, we don't have anything even vaguely like robots yet and maybe never will – '

'Now, Ivor, calm down, please. Technical men should not be subject to hysteria. I quite understand that you're worried about the loss of your livelihood, but I'm sure you can be retrained. Men of your calibre are hard to find.'

This was untrue, but since the argument was obviously getting nowhere, Ivor left, and tried a different tack: persuasion of senior men in his own branch of the field. That only got him nowhere in a different direction. The highest colleague he could reach was Enoch Amin, who had his own views:

'We'll never be redundant, Ivor. Powell doesn't know it, but ULTIMAC really *is* the ultimate in opportunities for us. Every computer in the world tied into it, and every one of them on the edge of taking sick overnight – to say nothing of the master machine itself. It's the design engineers like Powell who'll be put out of business; we'll be rushed off our feet.'

'But the whole damn system is supposed to be homeostatic – self-correcting!'

'All the more jobs for us. Did you ever hit a self-monitoring computer that worked? We'll be shooting all over the world, trying to find out which component went wrong where.' Amin stood up ecstatically, which, since he was half a foot taller than Ivor, made him seem as though he were about to go into orbit. 'And as for the Big One, my God, what an opportunity! Believe me, Ivor, we'll wind up the secret masters of the whole system. Wallowing in luxury, if we can just find the time off for it. And, of course, keep our focus firmly on the I.A.s.'

Ivor knew well enough that the I.A.s Amin was referring to made up an entirely different set than those Powell had invoked, and furthermore, constituted a trade secret. Neither set comforted him. He foresaw trouble on a massive scale, and neither Amin nor Powell could talk about it except in terms of keeping their jobs.

As mentioned, Ivor had a rudimentary social conscience,

but it was now clear to him that he had no pull. He had gone as high as he could in both directions. He went back to doing what he had been trained to do. He also fired his wives and his cats, gave up drinking and insofar as was possible, eating, and reduced his hobbies to the single one of saving his money at the highest interest rate he could find – specifically, in a bank whose computer, unbeknownst to anyone but himself, thought that the square root of $4·7$ was $0·68581425$, which was $0·001488$ too high.

He did not know why it thought so, and had no intention of trying to find out. Nor could he have, for that particular kind of bias was beyond his competence. But the effect of filling this parameter in this way upon the machine's way of compounding interest was satisfying enough so that six years later he was again eating well enough to gain a little weight back.

In fact, the whole next decade was idyllic for almost everyone. ULTIMAC was built, squarely across Niagara Falls – no lesser cooling system could have carried away its entropy loss alone. The gigantic building and its slave computers did everything they were supposed to do, and perfectly. By the end of that decade, if ULTIMAC decided to run the Amazon River backwards for twenty-four hours, or convert world math to the base twelve, or revive the railroad system, nobody argued. The decisions always worked, out to a margin of error so many decimal places to the right as to make Plancke's Constant look like a whole number, and a rather small one at that.

It put computermen of all stripes out of business, and all but a few politicians, too. Ivor didn't mind that either. Immediately after his one abortive venture into politics, he had taken the precaution of cutting his bank's computer off from ULTIMAC (under the guise of a routine check within his own sub-speciality) and as a result could also begin thinking about again taking in one cat (though, certainly, not yet a wife).

This tiny loss of input went unnoticed by ULTIMAC,

which recorded only what it was fed, not what it was not. Its glamourous, Government-chosen acronym bore no relation to how it actually worked: it was necessarily a topological computer, geared despite all its decimal places to the losing of some information it *did* have in the byways of its almost total connectivity. It compensated; it worked; that was enough. And it was particularly good, as predicted, at servicing itself; no human hand was asked to touch it from the moment it went on stream, and most certainly not Ivor's.

Nor would he have done so if asked. As far as he was concerned, Utopia had arrived. Besides, topology was not his sub-speciality – in fact, he knew less about it than he did about poetry – and in ten years of calculated idleness he had almost forgotten the sub-speciality itself. He had even given up worrying. He did remember the trade-secret I.A.s, since he had sworn a solemn oath to do so, but bearing them in mind had become a useless exercise. And as for keeping his eye out for remote sands in which to bury his head, Just In Case, that had retreated into complacent fantasy.

So it was nobody's fault but his own that when the glitch hit ULTIMAC, he was virtually next door to the monster and was hired, nay, ordered, to fix it. The rest of this story is very sad indeed, and since by its very nature is not stored in ULTIMAC or anywhere else, you may not wish to read on. It requires a lot of explanation, too, and neither sadness nor explanations are welcome in our present, real Utopia. But they meant a lot to him, back in those days, and justice must be served, even to him.

Hence: among the trade-secret Laws of Computerics to which Ivor was sworn were the following:

I) Tell the customer nothing about the machine, even if you know somethng about it. If he insists, give him an incomplete Xerox copy of the assembly instructions for next year's model. The head office will have insured that his present model is in-

complete and that delivery date for the missing component cannot be predicted. If by any chance the customer has a complete machine, the On-Off switch has been designed not to function more than one time in six, which is the last thing the customer will suspect.

II) When the machine malfunctions, blame the customer's programmers. The manufacturer will then send in its own programming team to re-train the customer's programmers, on the premises. This group is highly skilled in disagreeing with the customer's team, item by item and over a long period.

III) After an independent programming team has been called in and the impasse has been reached, you (the service engineer) will be asked to investigate the machine itself. Since no machine makes a record of where or why it has malfunctioned, your duties are:

a) disappearing into the machine for AS LONG AS POSSIBLE;

b) introducing a new malfunction which you then correct;

c) filing a long and incomprehensible report.

A good service engineer should also master the art of disagreeing with glacial impartiality with all three programming teams.

IV) By this time the guarantee will have expired. Notify the manufacturer to send a salesman to the customer with colourful brochures about the succeeding model. Never at any time even hint that the malfunction was actually inside the machine.

These Laws had once functioned very well, but none of them were of any use to Ivor when he was confronted with ULTI-MAC. The Fourth Law was particularly inappropriate, since there could not be any succeeding machine to tout. And he had been put on the job, of course, because of his wrong-headed public spirit; for though he hadn't pressed it very hard or very long, both Powell and Amin remembered that he had predicted that something would go wrong. It was a perfect syllogism: he had predicted it, he was a service engineer, he was the man to fix it: Q.E.D.

Of course he did know, in a gross way, what the malfunction was. In answer to school-children's questions, ULTIMAC had taken to printing out in the home answers which would have been of dubious suitability even to advanced medical students. This part of its operation had been shut down, but while it seemed minor on the surface, chill premonitions passed up and down the spines of Government when they remembered that ULTIMAC was running everything else, too.

'The next thing,' Powell told him grimly, 'might be banana oil from the water taps. Or something much worse. You were right all along, Ivor. Go to it.'

Okay. But how? Like all service engineers – inevitably, since no single man could know everything there was to know about computers – Ivor knew only one kind of fault to look for. When he actually found one such, he fixed it. When he didn't, he created one and then fixed that, in accordance with Clause B of the Third Law. That wouldn't work this time, either.

Superficially, he might have seemed just the man to deal with ULTIMAC, since his particular sub-speciality was storage-and-retrieval, which was where the machine was (up to now) going potty. But that was a layman's mistake, though a natural one to make even for Powell. ULTIMAC had a glitch: that is, also in strict accordance with the opening proposition of the Third Law, it had not recorded the cause of its own malfunction. Moreover, since the glitch was a slip-page in storage-and-retrieval, the chances were high that the machine had actively wiped out whole areas of other informa-tion which might – just might – have contained a clue or two.

His hand sweating on the grip of his overloaded tool kit, Ivor was reverently ushered through a low door no man had entered in ten years, and ULTIMAC slid it shut behind him with a gritty slam.

Except for the sound of Niagara Falls, muted by diversion through hundreds of thousands of channels to a delicate murmur, the huge building was almost silent. Occasionally, there would be a small salvo of clicking noises, as though Ivor's first wife had broken a string of beads; and once, briefly, he thought he heard a louder, harsher version of the water sound. The air was fresh, bone-dry and in gentle motion, now and then carrying a whiff of ozone, and less often of things of which he could only say that they were certainly not ozone.

Concrete corridors stretched away from him radially and confusingly, twitching around corners and out of sight in no apparent pattern. They bore painted code numbers, and Ivor had been given a map, but the reality was not so simple. The corridors had not been built for human traverse. They were even lower than the door, single-file narrow, and had rails running down their middles. Since he had to suspect the rails of being electrified, he at once found that his pace and posture had to be approximately that of a swan out of water, and frequently further complicated by switch-points wherever the corridors crossed. Also, there was a lot of static; his hair stood up like a corona in a brush discharge. Should he touch any metal at all . . . but he tried not to think about that.

He had not progressed very far when he heard the harsh water noise again, this time growing louder. At its climax, something very like a fictional robot appeared ahead of him from the right, turned smartly on the track points, and retreated down the same corridor he was waddling along. He was too startled to get a good look at it, but he had the impression that it was about his own height and width, was about three times as thick, and had about ten times as many appendages as he did. Also, it most certainly did not waddle. It drove, purposefully.

Here was a danger he should have foreseen. As a self-repairing machine of record size, ULTIMAC had to have its own servicing devices: slave mechanical equivalents of Ivor himself, mobile and able to reach every cranny of the edifice.

The corridors were designed for them. Moreover, should he encounter one, there would be no room for both of them, and it would be obviously hopeless to try to tell it to stop.

After that, his progress was further slowed, since at every intersection he checked the setting of the track-points, so that if one of the servos should come up behind him he would be able to jump aside in the direction it was *not* going to go. As a by-product, he promptly got lost. He wished fervently for a compass, but an ordinary magnetic one would have been whirlingly useless in this electronic maze, and a gyro-compass would have been too bulky – his tool-kit arms were aching already. However, he managed to retrace his steps with the map and start over from where he had gone wrong.

Not long after, he heard the noise again. This time he saw the machine much earlier, for it was coming directly towards him. He had plenty of time to retreat to a previous intersection, where, he found, the servo was not going to turn in either direction. His early spotting had been aided by the fact that on the front of the thing a red code-number glowed, like the display in a pocket calculator. As it passed, he was able to see that the numbers were indeed a display, inside a slot-like window.

Here was a problem a good deal simpler than the glitch, in that it was probably soluble. There seemed to be no reason to number the servos themselves, and even had there been one, painted lettering would have served. A display subject to change more reasonably suggested the gadget's temporary area of assignment. He checked the code he had seen against his map. Yes, there was such a combination, about a mile back and to one side of the route he had been following.

An idea so crafty smote him that he almost chuckled before he realized that he had to be dead silent, or be dead. After he stopped trembling, it still seemed like a good idea.

Why not hitch a ride? Or a series of them? Even if it made his course much more indirect, it would be faster in the long run, and just possibly safer, too.

He got back in motion on his own in the meantime. In an hour's further uncomfortable progress he saw three more servos, and studied them as carefully as possible. All those appendages made him nervous; he wanted to make very sure that the gadgets were oblivious of him. There was only one way to be certain of that, which was to stand in the path of one, just beyond where the points showed it would have to turn away from him – and keep a sharp eye for last-minute changes in the track setting. On the third encounter, he nerved himself up to trying it.

The machine did not even falter; and as it turned off, he saw at its back a lattice-like structure festooned with tools – replacement 'hands' for its many arms. He could cling to that; it would be uncomfortable, but anything would be better by now than this back-breaking swan gait.

At his first attempt, he dropped his kit while jumping. The next one, however, worked. The servo took him almost as far away in all directions from his goal as it was possible to go; but at least he had learned that the trick was possible. (All experiments, after all, require several stages.) After that, he checked the map, and jumped only on those machines whose smoky-red codes showed destinations nearer and nearer where he was supposed to be.

To an omniscient observer his course would have resembled a three-dimensional version of the Brownian movement, but he got there eventually, or almost. As he had expected, no servo ever turned up which was going directly to the lair of the glitch, because this was precisely the area in which ULTIMAC itself did not know it was in trouble. He had to waddle the last half mile.

Once arrived, however, he sat down and rested for a while, feeling sticky as his sweat dried in the dehydrated air, but in a faint glow of pride at his own cunning and courage. Above all, for the first time he felt safe. This was the one place in the whole building where he would not and could not be threatened by the servos. After his heart stopped pounding, he opened his kit and approached the faceplate of the children's answering service, Phillips screwdriver in hand.

He had extracted two bolts and was working on a third when all hell broke loose. It began with a nearly-supersonic whistle, fortissimo, which made him so dizzy that he dropped the screwdriver and nearly fell. While he was still staggering, the now-familiar roar of a servo grew over the other noise, and then he was grabbed from behind by all his available appendages at once, nose and ears included, and rushed out of the chamber.

ULTIMAC did not, by definition, know it had a glitch in storage-and-retrieval. But now it *had* spotted a gross malfunction there. It was Ivor Harrigan and his bag of tools.

The building, as has been remarked, had not been designed for any human presence, and if ULTIMAC had ever been programmed to accept a rare living repairman, that memory had been wiped out too – just the kind of glitch nobody would ever detect until too late. Instead, the computer treated him, urgently, as a misplaced component, and the first problem evidently turned out to be identifying the component and locating where in the machine it was supposed to fit.

This involved thrusting him into a sort of outsize coffin where he was probed, rotated, measured, tested for conductivity – painful, but luckily the very first low shock must have shown that nothing so bulky could be primarily a resistor – shape, transparency, terminal matchings (hair by hair), moving parts (an aerial ballet of his clothing and the contents of his kit), and many other characteristics beyond his detection, including, doubtless, radioactivity, Gauss level, and a series of X-rays. (But at least he was not subjected to chemical analysis.)

Short work was made of the tools themselves. They were familiar and were whisked away, doubtless to be put into some storage rack for use at need by a servo. They may have decided the issue, for after a pause – three or four minutes, almost an eternity for a computer and more than one for the now watch-less Ivor – ULTIMAC decided what kind of component Ivor himself was: a new model of servo-mechanism, potentially more useful than the ones that ran on tracks, but at present badly out of adjustment. (For example, the unnecessary complexity of that internal waveguide system . . .)

He came to this conclusion only when he found himself on a conveyor-belt, neatly spaced between two ordinary servos whose innards were being reworked by devices which extruded themselves from the walls of the tube the belt crawled along. These he managed to dodge. He could not, however, prevent himself from being repainted and dried, twice; all he could do was close his eyes and stop breathing while the sprays were on.

The third coat – as he recognized by the smell – was a coat of enamel. Inevitably, the next stop would be a baking oven, probably around the next turn of the belt.

But the servo in front of him had not needed repainting, and the belt split to carry it off to somewhere else. Ivor ducked after it, and found himself in what he supposed must be the robot equivalent of a recovery room.

Bent almost double, his paint cracking and peeling with every move, but without a gram of detectable metal anywhere upon him, Ivor sprinted until at last he found an exit. On the way, he disabled everything he recognized, and threw switches at random on everything he didn't. By the time he got out, ULTIMAC had become noisier than Niagara Falls had ever been, and three minutes later became the largest barrel ever to go over it.

To the end of his life, he was called Ivor the Glitch, and in history still is. He never got another job, either. But he still had his bank with the built-in error; and however he may have felt about it all, things are quieter around here now. There always had been people who had been uneasy at the thought that they might wake up tomorrow to find the Amazon River running backward.

Conversation on a Starship in Warpdrive

John Brosnan

Nick Nova, intergalactic adventurer and product of shoddy twenty-eighth-century artificial insemination techniques, entered the passenger lounge of the S.S. *Firebrand*. It was full of steam. He groped his way through it until he located an empty seat; as he slumped into it the steam cleared momentarily, enabling him to see the person in the seat next to him. It was a tall, thin naked man.

'Hot in here, isn't it?' said Nick. The man nodded, then said: 'But I prefer it here than in my cabin. It was snowing when I left.'

'Really?' said Nick. 'It snowed in mine yesterday. Bit of a nuisance.'

'Breaks the monotony though, which is the reason for it all, of course. Space travel was so dull before they came up with VICE – Variable Internal Climatic Environment.'

'Suppose so. Still, I can't help thinking there must be a better way of doing it.'

'Oh, they've tried everything, believe me. I've been wandering the star lanes all my life and I've seen it all. Once I travelled on a ship that was built to resemble an ancient galleon. The crew wore pirate costumes and had robot parrots stuck on their shoulders that squawked nautical obscenities non-stop. They even had the ship rock back and forth so you could get seasick.'

'Sounds similar to the one I was on. It was designed like the inside of a medieval castle. Everyone wore suits of armour and there was a torture chamber where the passengers could mangle android virgins.'

Silence followed and Nick took the opportunity to introduce

himself. The thin man shook his hand: 'My name's Fabius. Torno Fabius.'

'What's your line of business?' asked Nick.

'At the moment I'm a publisher, but I've been many things before that. Started out as a salesman for the "Orgasm of the Month Club" selling erotitape machines. Then I became a missionary.' He held up his hands, which had large holes through the palms. 'Crucified,' he explained. 'Occupational hazard. Never know how these primitive types will react to your preaching.'

'Must have been an interesting life, though?'

'Oh it was, at times. But it was never easy. You try and convert a whole planet within a set time-limit. The money wasn't that good, either, which was one of the reasons I gave the game up. That and the faulty equipment.'

'Faulty equipment?'

'Yeah. The stuff was always letting me down at crucial moments. I'd be walking across a lake, say, and whammo . . . a buoyancy shoe would give out and the next thing I knew I'd be treading water. But the worst example took place on the planet Renolt. I was due to perform the Ascension from the top of a hill. Should have been purely routine. A gravity sled, disguised as a cloud, drops down from the sky and I step onto it. Of course I'm controlling it from a radio device hidden in my robes. It rises, taking me with it. It's then supposed to carry me up to my ship which is hovering, invisible, several thousand feet overhead.

'But on this occasion, when I'm only about a hundred feet above the gaping crowd, one of the sled's gravity nullifiers cuts out. The sled immediately sags to one side and I fall off. Luckily I manage to grab hold of the edge of the sled but the scene is not a good one – the Messiah hanging helpless from the side of a tilted cloud. So I activate an android on board my ship which I keep for emergencies. It's disguised to look like the Virgin Mary and is jet-propelled. But as I am trying to fiddle with my remote-control device one-handed I drop it.

Next thing down comes the Virgin Mary with all jets blazing. She hurtles past me and ends up burying herself into fifty feet of bedrock. Scares hell out of the natives. I hear there's still a team of sociologists on Renolt observing the cultural after-effects.

'Then there was the time I was trying to convert a planet of asexual creatures. Finally got them to understand the concept of bi-sexuality but like a fool I told them about the Virgin Birth. Had to shoot my way out of one of their insane asylums.'

By now the steam had almost gone but it had begun to rain. Stewards started handing out umbrellas to the passengers.

'At least the service is good on this ship,' said Nova, unfurling his umbrella.

'It should be; the crew have nothing else to do.'

'I would have thought that running a ship this size would take a considerable amount of their time.'

Fabius laughed. 'The ship runs itself. It's completely automatic.'

'Are you sure? I went on one of those tours of the bridge and control room yesterday and everyone looked extremely busy.'

'It's a sham. All play-acting for the passengers' benefit. The control panels are all mock-ups, nothing but flashing lights and dummy buttons.'

'I didn't know that,' said Nova.

'Not many people do. Even a lot of the crew members themselves don't know. Adds to the authenticity of the whole thing. Like the engineer, the one they call Scotty. Notice how he's always covered with oil stains?'

Nova nodded.

'He puts them on himself from a can he keeps in his cabin. Liquid lubricants haven't been used on star-ships for centuries.'

'Why is he called "Scotty"?'

'God knows. It's one of those traditions dating back for centuries. Like the First Officer on a ship always having to wear pointed plastic ears.'

'Yes, I've often wondered about that,' said Nova.

Fabius suddenly bent down and opened a bag on the floor by his feet. 'I've got a bottle of home-made wine in here. Fancy a drop?'

'No thanks. Not just now.'

'How about something to read, then?' He handed Nova what appeared to be a number of different geometric shapes all fused together in one lump.

'What is it?' asked Nova.

'A book, of course,' said Fabius. 'My new line of business. Selling books.'

'It doesn't look much like a book.'

'It's a new development in the art of the novel, though the actual techniques have been known for centuries. In fact it started way back in the mid-twentieth. A famous writer began experimenting with the correlation of the psychic landscapes and the landscapes of the external world. As he himself put it: "At what point does the plane of intersection between two wooden cones become as sexually stimulating as the cleavage of a well-endowed woman?" '

Nova thought it over carefully. Finally he said: 'I can't remember ever being sexually stimulated by two wooden cones, no matter what their point of intersection.'

'Ah, perhaps not consciously, but subconsciously you were. Your subconscious reeks lust every time it sees two inter-secting cones.'

'No wonder I feel tired all the time.'

'You see,' said Fabius, 'words are inefficient symbols for the purpose of communication. Where once it took a writer many thousands of words to express himself satisfactorily, he can now achieve the same result with a single geometric shape. This object will evoke all the responses in your mind that an old-fashioned book once did.'

Nova was impressed. He stared hard at the 'book'.

'Had you read *War and Peace* before?'

'No,' said Nova.

'Well you have now.'

'I don't feel as if I have.'

'Naturally it takes time for it all to sink in. Your subconscious has to mull it over.'

'Have you got one with pictures?'

'Afraid not. But this one might be more to your liking. It's a science-fiction thriller about a beautiful girl who turns out to be an android full of tiny, warlike creatures who want to destroy humanity. The android goes around killing men by shooting laser beams out of her nipples. The hero of the book escapes a similar fate because he hears whispering coming from her stomach while they are making love, and he becomes suspicious.'

'I knew a girl with green nipples once,' said Nova. 'They glowed in the dark.'

'How about this one?' said Fabius, producing another object. 'This one has been banned on fifteen planets. One of the most obscene books ever written.'

Nova looked at it with interest, but remained disappointed. 'It doesn't do a thing for me.'

'Nothing at all? Don't you feel a little depraved? Somewhat corrupted?'

Nova shook his head. 'I'm sorry, but I prefer the old style of books better.'

'To be honest, so do I. But these are the things that are selling. What's worse, I hear that writers have evolved their profession even further. They're communicating directly with their readers now. You just call up your favourite author, settle on a fee, and he comes and lives with you for a couple of days. During that time he pours out his ideas to you. Cuts out the middle man completely.'

'Sounds terrible.'

'I agree,' said Fabius. 'The thought of having the authors I've met as house guests for any length of time is quite repulsive. Oh blast, it's beginning to snow again. I'll have to go and get dressed. See you later.'

'Been nice talking to you,' Nova said as Fabius got up hurriedly and left the room. A white card lay where he had been sitting, and Nova picked it up. It said: 'You have just been talking to the "Interesting Character Android" model 42B, with the compliments of the Captain. A product of "ANDROIDS UNLIMITED", the 42B model guarantees a fascinating conversation covering a wide range of topics. It is sure to be one of the most memorable encounters of your journey.'

The Alibi Machine
Larry Niven

McAllister left the party around eight o'clock.

'Out of tobacco,' he told his host apologetically. The police, if they got that far would discover that that had been a little white lie. There were other parties in Greenwich Village on a Saturday night, and he would be attending one in about – he estimated – twenty minutes.

He took the elevator down. There was a displacement booth in the lobby. He dropped a coin in the slot, smiling fleetingly at himself – he had almost forgotten to take coins – and dialled. A moment later he was outside his own penthouse door in Queens.

He had saved himself the time to let himself in by leaving his briefcase under a potted plant earlier this evening. He tipped the pot, picked up the briefcase and stepped back into the booth. His conservative paper business suit made him look as if he had just come from work and the briefcase completed the picture nicely.

He dialled three times. The first number took him to Kennedy International. The second to Los Angeles International. Long distance flicks required the additional equipment available only at what had once been airports: equipment to compensate for the difference in rotational velocity between different points on the Earth. The third number took him to Jacob Anderson's home in the high Sierras.

It was five o'clock here, and the summer sun was still high. McAllister found himself gasping as he left the booth. Why would Anderson want to live at eight thousand feet?

For the view, he supposed; and because Anderson, a freelance writer, did not have to leave his home as often as normal people did. But there was also his love of privacy . . . and distrust of people.

He rang the bell.

Anderson's look was more surprised than welcoming. 'It was tomorrow. After lunch, remember?'

'I know, but – ' McAllister hefted the briefcase. 'Your royalty accounts arrived this afternoon. A day earlier than we expected. I got to thinking, why not have it out now? Why let you go on thinking you've been cheated a day longer than – '

'Uh huh.' Anderson had an imposing scowl. He gave no indication that he was ready to change his mind – and McAllister had nothing to change it with anyway. Publishing companies had always fudged a little on their royalty statements. Sometimes they took a bit too much, and then a writer might rear back on his hind legs and demand an audit.

The difference here was that Brace Books didn't know what McAllister had been doing with Lucas Anderson's accounts.

'Let's just go over these papers,' he said with a trace of impatience.

Anderson nodded without enthusiasm, and stepped back, inviting him in.

Did he have company? A glance into the dining nook told McAllister that he did not. A dinner setting for one, laid out with mathematical precision by one or another of Anderson's machines. Anderson's house was a display case of labour saving devices.

How to get him into the living room? But Anderson was leading him there. It was not a big house, and a hostile publisher's assistant would not be invited into the semi-sacred writing room.

Anderson stopped in the middle of the room. 'Spread it on the coffee table.'

McAllister circled Anderson as he reached into the briefcase. His fingers brushed papers, and then the GyroJet, and suddenly his pulse was thundering in his ears. He was afraid.

He'd spent considerable time plotting this. He'd even typed outlines, as for a mystery novel, and burned them afterward. He could produce the royalty statements; they were there in his briefcase, though they would not stand up. Or . . . his hand, unseen within the briefcase, clenched into a fist.

He was between Anderson and the picture window when he produced the GyroJet.

The GyroJet: an ancient toy or weapon, depending. It was a rocket pistol, made during the 1960s, then discontinued. This one had been stolen from someone's house and later sold to McAllister, secretly, a full twelve years ago.

A rocket pistol. How could any former Buck Rogers fan have turned down a rocket pistol? He had never shown it to anyone. He had had the thought, even then, that it would be untraceable should he ever want to kill somebody.

The true weapon was the rocket slug. The gun looked like a toy; flimsy aluminium, perforated down the barrel. Anderson might have thought it was a toy . . . but Anderson was bright. He got the point immediately. He turned to run.

McAllister shot him twice in the back.

He left by the front door. He grinned as he passed the displacement booth. Fifteen years ago there had been people who put their displacement booths inside, in the living room, say. But it made burglaries much too easy.

The alibi machine, the newspapers had called it then. They still did. The advent of the displacement booths had produced one hell of a crime wave. When a man in say, Hawaii could commit murder in Chicago and be back in the time it would take him to visit the men's room, it did make things a bit difficult for the police. McAllister himself would be at a party in New York ten minutes from now. But first . . .

He walked around to the back of the house and stood a moment, looking into the picture window.

He'd thrown a paper tablecloth over Anderson's body. Glass particles on the body would be a giveaway. He'd take the tablecloth with him; and how were the police to know that it was the third bullet, rather than the first, that had shattered the picture window? But if it was the first bullet, then the killer must have been someone Anderson would not let into the house.

McAllister fired into the picture window.

Glass showered inward. There was the scream of an alarm.

McAllister stood rooted. It was a terrible sound, and in these quiet hills it would carry forever! He hadn't expected alarms. There must be a secondary system, continually in operation – Hell with it. McAllister ran into the house, picked up the tablecloth and ran out. Glass particles all over his shoes. Never mind. His shoes and everything else he was wearing were paper, and there was a change of clothing in the briefcase. He'd dump gun and all at the next number he dialled.

The altitude was getting to him. He was panting like a bloodhound when he closed the booth door and dialled. Los Angeles International, then a lakeside resort in New Mexico. The police could hardly search every lake in the country.

Nothing happened.

He dialled again. And again, while the alarm screamed to the hills, *Help! I am being robbed.* When his hand was shaking too badly to dial, he backed out of the glass door and stood looking at the booth.

This hadn't been in any of the outlines.

The booth wouldn't let him out. In all this vastness he was locked in, locked in with the body.

It was two hours before the helicopter from Fresno arrived. Even so, they made good speed. Only a police organization could get a copter in the air that fast. Who else dealt with situations in which one could not simply flick in?

The copter landed in front of the Anderson house, after some trouble picking it out of the wild landscape. Police Lieutenant Richard Donaho climbed out carefully as soon as the dust had stopped swirling. For the benefit of the pilot his face was unnaturally blank. The fear of death had taken him the instant the blades started whirling around, and it was only now leaving him.

With the motor off, the alarm from the house was an intolerable scream. Lieutenant Donaho moved around to the side of the machine, opened a hatch and switched in the portable JumpShift unit.

He stood back as men and equipment began pouring through. Uniformed men moved toward the house, spreading out. Donaho didn't interfere. He wasn't expecting anything startling. It was going to be cold burglary, the burglar vanished quite away.

It was a smallish one-storey house in a wild and beautiful setting, halfway up a mountain. The sun was still bright, though it had almost touched the western peaks. The sky was dark blue, almost lavender. Houses were scarce upslope, and far scarcer downslope. There were no roads. No roads at all. This place must have been uninhabited until twenty years ago, when JumpShift Inc. had revolutionized transportation.

The shrill of the alarm stopped.

In the sudden silence a policeman walked briskly from around the side of the house. 'Lieutenant!' he called. 'It's not burglary. It's murder. There's a dead man on the living room rug.'

'All right,' said Donaho. He called Homicide.

Captain Hennessey flicked in with the hot summer air of Fresno around him. It puffed out when he opened the door, and he felt the dry chill of the mountains. His ears popped. He stepped out of the belly of the copter, looking for the nearest man. 'Donaho! What's happening?'

Donaho nodded at the uniformed man, whose name was Fisher. Fisher said, 'It's around the back. Picture window shattered. Man inside, dead, with two holes in his back. That's as far as we've got. Want to come look, sir?'

'In a minute. What was wrong with the displacement booth? Never mind, I see it.'

It was obvious even from here. The displacement booth was a standard model, a glass cylinder rounded at the top, with a dial system set in the side. Its curved door was blocked open by a chunk of granite.

'So that's why you needed the copter,' said Hennessey. 'Hum.' He hadn't expected that.

It was an old trick. Any burglar knew enough to block the displacement booth door before trying to rob a house. If he set off an alarm the police couldn't flick in, and he could generally run next door and use the displacement booth there. But *here* –

'I wonder how he got out?' said Hennessey. 'He couldn't set the rock and then use the booth. Maybe he couldn't use the booth anyway. Some alarms lock the transmitter on the booth, so people can still flick in but nobody can flick out.'

Donaho shifted impatiently. This was a murder investigation, and he had not yet so much as seen the body.

Hennessey looked down a rocky, wooded slope, darkening with dusk. 'Hikers would call this leg-breaker country,' he said. 'But that's how he did it. There's no other way he could get out. When the booth wouldn't send him anywhere, he blocked the door open and set out for . . . hum.'

The nearest house was half a mile away. It was bigger than Anderson's house, with a pool and a stretch of lawn and a swing and a slide, all clearly visible in miniature from this vantage point.

'For there, I think. He'd rather go down than up. He'd have to circle that stretch of chaparel . . .'

'Captain, do you really think so? *I* wouldn't try walking through that.'

'You'd stay here and wait for the fuzz? It's not *that* bad. You'd make two miles an hour without a backpack. Hell, he might even have planned it this way. I hope he left footprints. We'll want to know if he wore hiking boots.' Hennessey scowled. 'Not that it'll do us any good. He could have reached the nearest house a good hour ago.'

'That doesn't mean he could use the booth. Someone might have seen him.'

'Hum. Right. Or . . . he might have broken an ankle anyway mightn't he? Donaho, get that copter up and start searching the area. We'll have someone in Fresno question the neighbours. With the alarm blaring like that, they might have been more than usually alert.'

Lieutenant Donaho had not greatly enjoyed his first helicopter flight, which had ended twenty minutes ago. Now he was in the air again, and the slender wings were beating round and round over his head, and the ground was an uncomfortable distance below.

'You don't like this much,' the pilot said perceptively. He was a stocky man of about forty.

'Not much,' Donaho agreed. It would have been nice if he could close his eyes, but he had to keep watching the scenery. There were trees a man could hide in, and a brook a man might have drunk from. He watched for movement; he watched for footprints. The scenery was both too close and too far down, and it wobbled dizzyingly.

'You're too young,' said the pilot. 'You young ones don't know anything about speed.'

Donaho was amused. 'I can go anywhere in the world at the speed of light.'

'Hell, that isn't *speed*. Ever been on a motorcycle?'

'*No.*'

'I was using a chopper when they started putting up the JumpShift booths all over the place. Man, it was wonderful. It was like all the cars just evaporated! It took years, but it didn't seem that way. They left all those wonderful freeways for just us. You know what the most dangerous thing was about riding a chopper? It was cars.'

'Yah.'

'Same with flying. I don't own a plane. God knows I haven't got the money, but I've got a friend who does. It's a lot more fun now we've got the airfields to ourselves. No more big planes. No more problem refuelling either. We used to worry about running out of gas.'

'Uh huh.' A thought struck Donaho. 'What do you know about off-the-road vehicles?'

'Not that much. They're still made. I can't think of one small enough to fit into a displacement booth, if that's what you're thinking.'

'I was. Hennessey thinks the killer might have set off the alarm deliberately. If he did, he might have brought an off-the-road vehicle along. Are you sure he couldn't get one into a booth?'

'No, I'm not.' The pilot looked down, considering. 'It's too damn steep for a ground-effect vehicle. He'd leave tyre tracks.'

'What would they look like?'

'Oh, God. You mean it, don't you? Look for two parallel lines, say three to six feet apart. Most tyres are corrugated, and you'd see that too.'

There was nothing like that in sight.

'Then, I know guys who might try to take a chopper across this. Might break their stupid necks, too, That'd leave a trail like a caterpillar track, but corrugated.'

'I can't believe anyone would walk across this. It looked like half a mile of bad stairs back there. And how would he get through those bushes?'

'Crawl. Not that I'd try it myself. But they don't want me for the gas chamber.' The pilot laughed. 'Can you see the poor bastard, standing in the booth, dialling and dialling – '

Lucas Anderson had been a big man. He had left a big corpse

sprawled across a sapphire-blue rug, his arms stretched way out, big hand clutching. They had been dragging a dead weight. One of the holes in his back was high up, just over the spine.

And men moved about him, doing things that would not help him and probably would not catch his killer.

Someone had come here expressly to kill Lucas Anderson. He would have some connection with him, in business or friendship or enmity. He might have left traces of himself, and if he had, these men would find him.

But the alibi machine might have put him anywhere by now. With a valid passport he could be in Algiers or Moscow.

Anderson's bookshelf of his own works showed some science fiction titles. His killer *could* have been a spaceman – and then he could be in Mars orbit by now, or moving toward Jupiter at lightspeed as a kind of superneutrino.

Yet they were learning things about him.

The cleaning machines had come on as soon as the alarm had been switched off. An alert policeman had got to them before they could do anything about the mess.

There was no glass on the body.

There was no glass under the body either.

'Now, that's not particularly odd,' the man in the white coat said to Hennessey. 'I mean, the pattern of explosion might have done that. But it means we can't say one way or another.'

'He could have been dead when the shot was fired.'

'Sure, or the other way around. No glass on him could mean he came running in when he heard all the noise. Just a minute,' the man in the white coat said quickly, and he stooped far down to examine Anderson's big shoes with a magnifying glass. 'I was wrong. No glass here.'

'Hum, Anderson must have let him in. Then he shot out the window to fox us, and set off the alarm. That wasn't too bright.' In a population of three hundred million Americans you could usually find a dozen suspects for any given murder victim. An intelligent killer would simply risk it.

Someday, Hennessey thought when the black mood was on him, someday murder would be an accepted thing. It was that hard to stop. But this one might not have escaped yet . . .

'I'd like to get the body to the lab,' said the man in the white coat. 'Can't do an autopsy here. I want to probe for the bullets. They'd tell us how far away he was shot from, if we can get a gun like it, to do test firing.'

'If? Unusual gun?'

The man laughed. 'Very. The slug in the wall was a solid fuel rocket, four nozzles the size of pinholes, angled to spin the thing. Impact like a ·45.'

'Hum.' Hennessey asked of nobody in particular, 'Get any footprints?'

Someone answered. 'Yessir, in the grass outside. Paper shoes. Small feet. Definitely not Anderson's.'

'Paper shoes.' Could he have planned to hike out? Brought a pair of hiking boots to change into? But it began to look like the killer hadn't planned anything so elaborate.

The dining setup would indicate that Anderson hadn't been expecting visitors. If premeditated murder could be called casual, this had been a casual murder, except for the picture window. Police had searched the house and found no sign of theft. Later they could learn what enemies Anderson had made in life. For now –

For now, the body should be moved to Fresno. 'Call the copter back,' Hennessey told someone. They'd need the portable JumpShift unit in the side.

When the wind from the copter had died Hennessey stepped forward with the rest, with the team that carried the stretcher. He asked of Donaho, 'Any luck?'

'None,' said Lieutenant Donaho. He climbed out, stood a moment to feel solid ground beneath his feet. 'No footprints, no tracks, nobody hiding where we could see him. There's a lot of woods where he could be hiding, though. Look, it's after sunset, Captain. Get us an infrared scanner and we'll go up again when it gets dark.'

'Good.' More time for the killer to move . . but there were only half a dozen houses he could try for, Hennessey thought. He could get permission from the owners to turn off their booths for a while. Maybe.

'But I don't believe it,' Donaho was saying. 'Nobody could travel a mile through that. And the word from Fresno is that the only unoccupied house is two miles off to the side!'

'Never a boy scout, were you?'

'No. Why?'

'We used to hike these hills with thirty pounds of backpack. Still . . . hum.' He seemed to be studying Donaho's face. 'Is Anderson's booth back in operation?'

'Yes, You were right, Captain. It was hooked to the alarm.'

'Then we can send the copter home and use that. Listen, Donaho, I may have been going at this wrong. Let me ask you something . . .'

Most of the police were gone by ten. The body was gone. There was fingerprint powder on every polished surface, and glass all over the living room. Hennessey and Donaho and the uniformed man named Fisher sat at the dining table, drinking coffee made in the Anderson kitchen.

'Guess I'll be going home,' Donaho said presently. He made no reference to what they had planned.

They watched through the window as Lieutenant Donaho, brilliantly lighted, vanished within the glass booth.

After that they drank coffee, and talked, and watched. The stars were very bright.

It was almost midnight before anything happened. Then, a rustling sound . . . and something burst into view from upslope, a shadowy figure in full flight. It was in the displacement booth before Hennessey and Fisher had even reached the front door.

The booth light showed every detail of a lean dark man in a rumpled paper business suit, one hand holding a briefcase, the other dialling frantically. Dialling again, while one eye in a shyly averted face watched two armed men strolling up to the booth.

'No use,' Hennessey called pleasantly. 'Lieutenant Donaho had it cut off as soon as he flicked out.'

The man released a ragged sigh.

'We want the gun.'

The man considered. Then he handed out the briefcase. The gun was in there. The man came out after it. He had a beaten look.

'Where were you hiding?' Hennessey asked.

'Up there in the bushes, where I could see you. I knew you'd turn the booth back on sooner or later.'

'Why didn't you just walk down to the nearest house?'

The lean man looked at him curiously. Then he looked down across the black slope, to where a spark of light showed one window still glowing in a distant house. 'Oh, my God. I never thought of that.'

Emergency Society
Uta Frith

It was emergency time again. Everybody got together their red-and-white-striped gear, their heart-shaped First Aid boxes, their miniature emergency weapons kits. Some people also reached down such extras as umbrellas, gas masks, diving suits, asbestos overalls, spiked shoes, stilts, and the like – but these were optional.

Everybody loved emergency time, especially the children. It was a time for dressing up, for action, and there was always the chance that something absolutely new, something really surprising would happen.

Spinelli, recently retired from public office, chose to stay at home, close beside his radio and his huge, glowing television set. On-the-spot newsflashes were being transmitted continuously. The excitement was terrific, as it always was when emergency time had been announced.

What would it be this time? Bets were placed, computers and public opinion polls were consulted. Astrologers pronounced remarkable divinations, newspapers gave authoritative reports from special correspondents. Intuitions were widely exchanged. Everybody, but everybody, had a pet hypothesis. Some people firmly believed that the worst – that is, whatever they feared the most – would undoubtedly come to pass. Some maintained the belief that it would happen to the others, not to them. A large group was convinced that punishment was imminent for all wrongdoers and that general repentance should prevail.

As Spinelli remembered from his own youth, such intense and active entertainment was no more than dreamed of by the

theatrical and cinema industries of the distant past. The anticipation alone counted for more than any circus spectacular
presented by a Roman emperor. The people themselves were
in the arena, arbitrary spectators and actors, victims or victors
determined by the mysterious plans of the Council.

With millions of other viewers, Spinelli watched flashbacks
and highlights of emergencies of the last decade. He knew, all
the viewers knew, that each time they survived unscathed they
formed the true emergency society. Twice, Spinelli himself
had been decorated as a hero: in the Great Flood he had
organized a rescue fleet to pluck scores of people from the
foaming torrents, and during the Locust Plague he had flown
insecticide into the afflicted areas at considerable risk to his
own safety.

Emergency, of course, was not without its lighter side.
Spinelli laughed and laughed again at the well-loved scenes
from the Racoon Invasion, when hundreds of racoons had
been parachuted into suburban gardens, and the Custard Pie
Orgy, when pies had been flung by the million in one huge
comedy.

There were dramatic sequences, too, from the day when
Russian roulette was played by every hundredth person in
the telephone directory, and there were pictures of the foot-
and-mouth disease, the collapsing blocks of flats, the special
earthquakes, and so on. The television interviewer approached
a man swathed in bearskins: 'So you think there'll be a new
Ice Age this time?' 'It was bound to happen sooner or later,'
the man replied, shrugging the fur around his ears, 'I can
already feel the cold, can't you?' In the background, a wild
figure could be glimpsed shouting that the plagues of Egypt
were about to return.

Spinelli liked the news best on these occasions – better, if
the truth be told, than the spectacle itself. He was looking
forward to all the papers the next day; the heroes would be
announced, the victims mourned. Even if there was grief and
loss in some places, the following week would be celebrated

by all the happy people who had truly emerged. It was miraculous how human ingenuity, organization and adaptability saved the community from disaster every time. No disaster was ever bad enough to make any difference to economic expansion or population increase.

'Hard times,' a businessman observed on the cascading screen not far from Spinelli's nose, 'have always been a blessing to us. People get together and help each other. All the petty squabbles of weeks past are forgotten when we put on our emergency kit. United we are strong.' He was leading his entire staff towards one of the football stadiums, where whole communities would often gather to watch, entranced, the events unfolding on the giant televideo panoramas.

How true, Spinelli thought. He himself was a founder member of the party that had introduced emergency. 'Already fifty years ago,' said the television interviewer, 'psychologists proved that the destructive impulses in man, allowed for centuries to burst out in unmotivated violence and irrational acts of warfare, could be channelled into useful paths. Creative energy, intelligence, presence of mind, courage, honour, selfless sacrifice, discipline – once these qualities were almost forgotten. But now, thanks to emergency, they have returned to enrich our civilization.'

Spinelli recalled his student days when, longing for purpose and excitement, he and his friends would stage demonstrations and riots in order to capture the flavour of real and personal involvement. How often they had been stunned at the indifference they had encountered! Yes, it had all changed now; the party had helped to bring sense and meaning to everyday life.

It was in this moment of contentment that Spinelli was destined to take the role of victim for the first and last time in his existence. As in millions of other homes, his television set exploded.

Look, You Think You've Got Troubles?

Carol Carr

To tell you the truth, in the old days we would have sat shivah for the whole week. My so-called daughter gets married, my own flesh and blood, and not only he doesn't look Jewish, he's not even human.

'Papa,' she says to me, two seconds after I refuse to speak to her again in my entire life, 'if you know him you'll love him, I promise.' So what can I answer – the truth, like I always tell her: 'If I know him I'll vomit, that's how he affects me. I can help it? He makes me want to throw up on him.'

With silk gloves you have to handle the girl, just like her mother. I tell her what I feel, from the heart, and right away her face collapses into a hundred cracks and water from the Atlantic Ocean makes a soggy mess out of her paper sheath. And that's how I remember her after six months – standing in front of me, sopping wet from the tears and making me feel like a monster – me – when all the time it's her you-should-excuse-the-expression husband who's the monster.

After she's gone to live with him (new Horizon Village, Crag City, Mars), I try to tell myself it's not me who has to – how can I put it? – deal with him intimately; if she can stand it, why should I complain? It's not like I need somebody to carry on the business; my business is to enjoy myself in my retirement. But who can enjoy? Sadie doesn't leave me alone for a minute. She calls me a criminal, a worthless no-good with gallstones for a heart.

'Hector, where's your brains?' she says, having finally given up on my emotions. I can't answer her. I just lost my daughter, I should worry about my brains, too? I'm silent as the grave.

I can't eat a thing. I'm empty – drained. It's as though I'm waiting for something to happen, but I don't know what. I sit in a chair that folds me up like a bee in a flower and rocks me to sleep with electronic rhythms when I feel like sleeping, but who can sleep? I look at my wife and I see Lady Macbeth. Once I caught her whistling as she pushed the button for her bath. I fixed her with a look like an icicle tipped with arsenic.

'What are you so happy about? Thinking of your grand-children with the twelve toes?'

She doesn't flinch. An iron woman.

When I close my eyes, which is rarely, I see our daughter when she was fourteen years old, with skin just beginning to go pimply and no expression yet on her face. I see her walking up to Sadie and asking her what she should do with her life now she's filling out, and my darling Sadie, my life's mate, telling her why not marry a freak; you got to be a beauty to find a man here, but on Mars you shouldn't know from so many fish. 'I knew I could count on you, Mama,' she says, and goes ahead and marries a plant with legs.

Things go on like this – impossible – for months. I lose twenty pounds, my nerves, three teeth and I'm on the verge of losing Sadie, when one day the mailchute goes ding-dong and it's a letter from my late daughter. I take it by the tips of two fingers and bring it into where my wife is punching ingredients for the gravy I won't eat tonight.

'It's a communication from one of your relatives.'

'Oh-oh-oh.' My wife makes a grab for it, meanwhile punching CREAM-TOMATO-SAUCE-BEEF DRIPPINGS. No wonder I have no appetite.

'I'll give it to you on one condition only,' I tell her, holding it out of her trembling reach. 'Take it into the bedroom and read it to yourself. Don't even move your lips for once; I don't want to know. If she's God forbid dead, I'll send him a sympathy card.'

Sadie has a variety of expressions but the one thing they

have in common is they all wish me misfortune in my present and future life.

While she's reading the letter I find suddenly I have nothing to do. The magazines I read already. Breakfast I ate (like a bird). I'm all dressed to go out if I felt like, but there's nothing outside I don't have inside. Frankly, I don't feel like myself – I'm nervous. I say a lot of things I don't really intend and now maybe this letter comes to tell me I've got to pay for my meanness. Maybe she got sick up there; God knows what they eat, the kind of water they drink, the creatures they run around with. Not wanting to think about it too much, I go over to my chair and turn it on to brisk massage. It doesn't take long till I'm dreaming (fitfully).

I'm someplace surrounded by sand, sitting in a baby's crib and bouncing a diapered kangaroo on my knee. It gurgles up at me and calls me grandpa and I don't know what I should do. I don't want to hurt its feelings, but if I'm a grandpa to a kangaroo, I want no part of it; I only want it should go away. I pull out a dime from my pocket and put it into its pouch. The pouch is full of tiny insects which bite my fingers. I wake up in a sweat.

'Sadie! Are you reading, or rearranging the sentences? Bring it in here and I'll see what she wants. If it's a divorce, I know a lawyer.'

Sadie comes into the room with her I-told-you-so waddle and gives me a small wet kiss on the cheek – a gold star for acting like a mensch. So I start to read it, in a loud monotone so she shouldn't get the impression I give a damn:

'Dear Daddy, I'm sorry for not writing sooner. I suppose I wanted to give you a chance to simmer down first.'

(Ingrate! Does the sun simmer down?)

'I know it would have been inconvenient for you to come to the wedding, but Mor and I hoped you would maybe send us a letter just to let us know you're okay and still love me, in spite of everything.'

Right at this point I feel a hot sigh followed by a short but wrenching moan.

'Sadie, get away from my neck. I'm warning you . . .'

Her eyes are going flick-a-fleck over my shoulder, from the piece of paper I'm holding to my face, back to the page, flick-a-fleck, flick-a-fleck.

'All right, already,' she shoo-shoos me. 'I read it, I know what's in it. Now it's your turn to see what kind of a lousy father you turned out to be.' And she waddles back into the bedroom, shutting the door extra careful, like she's handling a piece of snow-white velvet.

When I'm certain she's gone, I sit myself down on the slab of woven dental floss my wife calls a couch and press a button on the arm that reads SEMI-CL.: FELDMAN TO FRIML. The music starts to slither out from the speaker under my left armpit. The right speaker is dead and buried and the long narrow one at the base years ago got drowned from the dog, who to this day hasn't learned to control himself when he hears 'Desert Song.'

This time I'm lucky; it's a piece by Feldman that comes on. I continue to read, calmed by the music.

'I might as well get to the point, Papa, because for all I know you're so mad you tore up this letter without even reading it. The point is that Mor and I are going to have a baby. Please, please don't throw this into the disintegrator. It's due in July, which gives you over three months to plan the trip up here. We have a lovely house, with a guest room that you and Mama can stay in for as long as you want.'

I have to stop here to interject a couple of questions, since my daughter never had a head for logic and it's my strong point.

First of all, if she were in front of me in person right now I would ask right off what means 'Mor and I are going to have a baby.' Which? Or both? The second thing is, when she refers to it as 'it' is she being literal or just uncertain? And just one more thing and then I'm through for good: Just how lovely can a guest room be that has all the air piped in and you can't even see the sky or take a walk on the grass because there is no grass, only simulated this and substituted that?

All the above notwithstanding, I continued to read:

'By the way, Papa, there's something I'm not sure you understand. Mor, you may or may not know, is as human as you and me, in all the important ways – and frankly a bit more intelligent.'

I put down the letter for a minute just to give the goose-bumps a chance to fly out of my stomach ulcers before I go on with her love and best and kisses and hopes for seeing us soon, Lorinda.

I don't know how she manages it, but the second I'm finished, Sadie is out of the bedroom and breathing hard.

'Well, do I start packing or do I start packing? And when I start packing, do I pack for us or do I pack for me?'

'Never. I should die three thousand deaths, each one with a worse prognosis.'

It's a shame a company like Interplanetary Aviation can't afford, with the fares they charge, to give you a comfortable seat. Don't ask how I ever got there in the first place. Ask my wife – she's the one with the mouth. First of all, they only allow you three pounds of luggage, which if you're only bringing clothes is plenty, but we had a few gifts with us. We were only planning to stay a few days and to sublet the house was Sadie's idea, not mine.

The whole trip was supposed to take a month, each way. This is one reason Sadie thought it was impractical to stay for the weekend and then go home, which was the condition on which I'd agreed to go.

But now that we're on our way, I decide I might as well relax. I close my eyes and try to think of what the first meeting will be like.

'How.' I put up my right hand in a gesture of friendship and trust. I reach into my pocket and offer him beads.

But even in my mind he looks at me blank, his naked pink antennas waving in the breeze like a worm's underwear. Then I realize there isn't any breeze where we're going. So they stop waving and wilt.

I look around in my mind. We're alone, the two of us, in the middle of a vast plain, me in my business suit and him in his green skin. The scene looks familiar, like something I had experienced, or read about . . . 'We'll meet at Philippi,' I think, and stab him with my sword.

Only then am I able to catch a few winks.

The month goes by. When I begin to think I'll never remember how to use a fork, the loudspeaker is turned on and I hear this very smooth, modulated voice, the tranquillized tones of a psychiatrist sucking glycerine, telling us it's just about over, and we should expect a slight jolt upon landing.

That slight jolt starts my life going by so fast I'm missing all the good parts. But finally the ship is still and all you can hear are the wheezes and sighs of the engines – the sounds remind me of Sadie when she's winding down from a good argument. I look around. Everybody is very white. Sadie's five fingers are around my upper arm like a tourniquet.

'We're here,' I tell her. 'Do I get a hacksaw or can you manage it yourself?'

'Oh, my goodness.' She loosens her grip. She really looks a mess – completely pale, not blinking, not even nagging.

I take her by the arm and steer her into customs. All the time I feel that she's a big piece of unwilling luggage I'm smuggling in. There's no cooperation at all in her feet and her eyes are going every which way.

'Sadie, shape up!'

'If you had a little more curiosity about the world you'd be a better person,' she says tolerantly.

While we're waiting to be processed by a creature in a suit like ours who surprises me by talking English, I sneak a quick look around.

It's funny. If I didn't know where we are I'd think we're in the back yard. The ground stretches out pure green, and it's only from the leaflet they give you in the ship to keep your mind off the panic that I know it's 100 per cent Acrispan we're looking at, not grass. The air we're getting smells good, too, like fresh-cut flowers, but not too sweet.

By the time I've had a good look and a breathe, what's-its-name is handing us back our passports with a button that says to keep Mars beautiful don't litter.

I won't tell you about the troubles we had getting to the house, or the misunderstanding about the tip, because to be honest I wasn't paying attention. But we do manage to make it to the right door, and considering that the visit was a surprise, I didn't really expect they would meet us at the airport. My daughter must have been peeking, though, because she's in front of us even before we have a chance to knock.

'Mother!' she says, looking very round in the stomach. She hugs and kisses Sadie, who starts bawling. Five minutes later, when they're out of the clinch, Lorinda turns to me, a little nervous.

You can say a lot of things about me, but basically I'm a warm person, and we're about to be guests in this house, even if she is a stranger to me. I shake her hand.

'Is he home, or is he out in the back yard, growing new leaves?'

Her face (or what I can see of it through the climate adapter) crumbles a little at the chin line, but she straightens it out and puts her hand on my shoulder.

'Mor had to go out, Daddy – something important came up – but he should be back in an hour or so. Come on, let's go inside.'

Actually there's nothing too crazy about the house, or even interesting. It has walls, a floor and a roof, I'm glad to see, even a few relaxer chairs, and after the trip we just had, I sit down and relax. I notice my daughter is having a little trouble looking me straight in the face, which is only as it should be, and it isn't long before she and Sadie are discussing pregnancy, gravitational exercise, labour, hospitals, formulas and sleep-taught toilet training. When I'm starting to feel that I'm getting over-educated, I decide to go into the kitchen and make myself a bite to eat. I could have asked them for a little something but I don't want to interfere with their first conversation. Sadie has all engines going and is interrupting four times a sentence, which is exactly the kind of game they always had back home – my daughter's goal is to say one complete thought out loud. If Sadie doesn't spring back with a non sequitur, Lorinda wins that round. A full-fledged knockout with Sadie still champion is when my daughter can't get a sentence in for a week. Sometimes I can understand why she went to Mars.

Anyway, while they're at the height of their simultaneous monologues, I go quietly off to the kitchen to see what I can dig up. (Ripe parts of Mor, wrapped in plastic? Does he really regenerate, I wonder? Does Lorinda fully understand how he works or one day will she make an asparagus omelet out of one of his appendages, only to learn that's the part that doesn't grow back? 'Oh, I'm so *sorry*,' she says. 'Can you ever forgive me?')

The refrigerator, though obsolete on Earth, is well stocked – fruits of a sort, steaks, it seems, small chicken-type things that might be stunted pigeons. There's a bowl of a brownish, creamy mess – I can't even bring myself to smell it. Who's hungry, anyway, I think. The rumbling in my stomach is the symptom of a father's love turning sour.

I wander into the bedroom. There's a large portrait of Mor hanging on the wall – or maybe his ancestor. Is it true that instead of hearts, Martians have a large avocado pip? There's a rumour on Earth that when Martians get old they start to turn brown at the edges, like lettuce.

There's an object on the floor and I bend down and pick it up. A piece of material – at home I would have thought it was a man's handkerchief. Maybe it is a handkerchief. Maybe they have colds like us. They catch a germ, the sap rises to combat the infection, and they have to blow their stamens. I open up a drawer to put the piece of material in (I like to be neat), but when I close it, something gets stuck. Another thing I can't recognize. It's small, round and either concave or convex, depending on how you look at it. It's made of something black and shiny. A cloth bowl? What would a vegetable be doing with a cloth bowl? Some questions are too deep for me, but what I don't know I eventually find out – and not by asking, either.

I go back to the living room.

'Did you find anything to eat?' Lorinda asks. 'Or would you like me to fix – '

'Don't even get up,' Sadie says quickly. 'I can find my way around any kitchen, I don't care whose.'

'I'm not hungry. It was a terrible trip. I thought I'd never wake up from it in one piece. By the way, I heard a good riddle on the ship. What's round and black, either concave or convex, depending on how you look at it, and made out of a shiny material?'

Lorinda blushed. 'A skullcap? But that's not funny.'

'So who needs funny? Riddles have to be a laugh a minute all of a sudden? You think Oedipus giggled all the way home from seeing the Sphinx?'

'Look, Daddy, I think there's something I should tell you.'

'I think there are all sorts of things you should tell me.'

'No, I mean about Mor.'

'Who do you think *I* mean, the grocery boy? You elope with a cucumber from outer space and you want I should be satisfied because he's human in all the important ways? What's important – that he sneezes and hiccups? If you tell me he snores, I should be ecstatic? Maybe he sneezes when he's happy and hiccups when he's making love and snores because it helps him think better. Does that make him human?'

'Daddy, *please*.'

'Okay, not another word.' Actually I'm starting to feel quite guilty. What if she has a miscarriage right on the spot? A man like me doesn't blithely torture a pregnant woman, even if she does happen to be his daughter. 'What's so important it can't wait till later?'

'Nothing, I guess. Would you like some chopped liver? I just made some fresh.'

'What?'

'Chopped liver – you know, chopped liver.'

Oh yes, the ugly mess in the refrigerator. 'You made it, that stuff in the bowl?'

'Sure. Daddy, there's something I really have to tell you.'

She never does get to tell me, though, because her husband walks in, bold as brass.

I won't even begin to tell you what he looks like. Let me just say he's a good dream cooked up by Mary Shelley. I won't go into it, but if it gives you a small idea, I'll say that his head is shaped like an acorn on top of a stalk of broccoli. Enormous blue eyes, green skin and no hair at all except for a small blue round area on top of his head. His ears are adorable. Remember Dumbo the Elephant? Only a little smaller – I never exaggerate, even for effect. And he looks boneless, like a fillet.

My wife, God bless her, I don't have to worry about; she's a gem in a crisis. One look at her son-in-law and she faints dead away. If I didn't know her better, if I wasn't absolutely certain that her simple mind contained no guile, I would have sworn she did it on purpose, to give everybody something to fuss about. Before we know what's happening, we're all in a tight, frantic conversation about what's the best way to bring her round. But while my daughter and her husband are in the bathroom looking for some deadly chemical, Sadie opens both eyes at once and stares up at me from the floor.

'What did I miss?'

'You didn't miss anything – you were only unconscious for fifteen seconds. It was a cat nap, not a coma.'

'Say hello, Hector. Say hello to him or so help me I'll close my eyes for good.'

'I'm very glad to meet you, Mr Trumbnick,' he says. I'm grateful that he's sparing me the humiliation of making the first gesture, but I pretend I don't see the stalk he's holding out.

'Smutual,' I say.

'I beg your pardon?'

'Smutual. How are you? You look better than your pictures.' He does, too. Even though his skin is green, it looks like the real thing up close. But his top lip sort of vibrates when he talks, and I can hardly bear to look at him except sideways.

'I hear you had some business this afternoon. My daughter never did tell me what your line is, uh, Morton.'

'Daddy, his name is Mor. Why don't you call him Mor?'

'Because I prefer Morton. When we know each other better I'll call him something less formal. Don't rush me, Lorinda; I'm still getting adjusted to the chopped liver.'

My son-in-law chuckles and his top lip really goes crazy. 'Oh, were you surprised? Imported meats aren't a rarity here, you know. Just the other day one of my clients was telling me about an all-Earth meal he had at home.'

'Your client?' Sadie asks. 'You wouldn't happen to be a lawyer?' (My wife amazes me with her instant familiarity. She could live with a tyrannosaurus in perfect harmony. First she faints, and while she's out cold everything in her head that was strange becomes ordinary and she wakes up a new woman.)

'No, Mrs Trumbnick. I'm a – '

' – rabbi, of course,' she finishes. 'I knew it. The minute Hector found that skullcap I knew it. Him and his riddles. A skullcap is a skullcap and nobody not Jewish would dare wear one – not even a Martian.' She bites her lip but recovers like a pro. 'I'll bet you were out on a Bar Mitzvah – right?'

'No, as a matter of fact – '

' – a Bris. I knew it.'

She's rubbing her hands together and beaming at him. 'A Bris, how *nice*. But why didn't you tell us, Lorinda? Why would you keep such a thing a secret?'

Lorinda comes over to me and kisses me on the cheek, and

I wish she wouldn't because I'm feeling myself go soft and I don't want to show it.

'Mor isn't *just* a rabbi, Daddy. He converted because of me and then found there was a demand among the colonists. But he's never given up his own beliefs, and part of his job is to minister to the Kopchopees who camp outside the village. That's where he was earlier, conducting a Kopchopee menopausal rite.'

'A what!'

'Look, to each his own,' says my wife with the open mind. But me, I want facts, and this is getting more bizarre by the minute.

'Kopchopee. He's a Kopchopee priest to his own race and a rabbi to ours, and that's how he makes his living. You don't feel there's a contradiction between the two, do you, Morton?'

'That's right. They both pray to a strong silent god, in different ways of course. The way my race worships, for instance – '

'Listen, it takes all kinds,' says Sadie.

'And the baby, whatever it turns out to be – will it be a Choptapi or a Jew?'

'Jew, shmoo,' Sadie says with a wave of dismissal. 'All of a sudden it's Hector the Pious – such a megilla out of a molehill.' She turns away from me and addresses herself to the others, like I've just become invisible. 'He hasn't seen the inside of a synagogue since we got married – what a rain that night – and now he can't take his shoes off in a house until he knows its race, colour and creed.' With a face full of fury, she brings me back into her sight. 'Nudnick, what's got into you?'

I stand up straight to preserve my dignity. 'If you'll excuse me, my things are getting wrinkled in the suitcase.'

Sitting on my bed (with my shoes on), I must admit I'm feeling a little different. Not that Sadie made me change my mind. Far from it; for many years now her voice is the white sound that lets me think my own thoughts. But what I'm realizing more and more is that in a situation like this a girl needs a father, and what kind of a man is it who can't sacrifice his personal feelings for his only daughter? When she was going out with Herbie the Haemophiliac and came home crying it had to end because she was afraid to touch him, he might bleed, didn't I say pack your things, we're going to Grossingers Venus for three weeks? When my twin brother Max went into kitchen sinks, who was it that helped him out at only four per cent? Always, I stood ready to help my family. And if Lorinda ever needed me, it's now when she's pregnant by some religious maniac. Okay – he makes me retch, so I'll talk to him, with a tissue over my mouth. After all, in a world that's getting smaller all the time, it's people like me who have to be bigger to make up for it, no?

I go back to the living room and extend my hand to my son-in-law the cauliflower. (Feh.)

A Delightful Comedic Premise
Barry N. Malzberg

Dear Mr Malzberg:

I wonder if you'd be interested in writing – on a semi-commissioned basis, of course – a funny short-story or nove-lette? Although the majority of your work, at least the work which I have read, is characterized by a certain gloom, a blackness, a rather despairing view of the world, I am told by people who represent themselves to be friends of yours that you have, in private, a delightful sense of humour which over-rides your melancholia and makes you quite popular at small parties. I am sure you would agree that science fiction, at least at present, has all the despair and blackness which its readers can stand, and if you could come in with a light-hearted story, we would not only be happy to publish it, it might start you on a brand-new career. From these same friends I am given to understand that you are almost thirty-four years of age, and surely you must agree that despair is harder and harder to sustain when you move into a period of your life where it becomes personally imminent; in other words, you are moving now into the Heart Attack Zone.

Dear Editor:

Thank you very much for your letter and for your interest in obtaining from me a light-hearted story. It so happens that you and my friends have discovered what I like to think of as My Secret . . . that I am not a despairing man at all but rather one with a delicious if somewhat perverse sense of humour, who sees the comedy in the human condition and only turns out the black stuff because it is now fashionable and the word rates, at all lengths, must be sustained.

I have had in mind for some time writing a story about a man, let me call him Jack, who is able to re-evoke the sights and sounds of the 1950s in such a concrete and viable fashion that he is actually able to *take* people back into the past, both individually and in small tourist groups. (This idea is not completely original; Jack Finney used it in *Time And Again*, and of course this chestnut has been romping or, I should say, dropping around the field for forty years, but hear me out.) The trouble with Jack is that he is not able to re-evoke the more fashionable and memorable aspects of the 1950s, those which are so much in demand in our increasingly perilous and confusing times, but instead can recover only the failures the not-quite-successes, the aspects-that-never-made-it. Thus he can take himself and companions not to Ebbets Field, say, where the great Dodger teams of the 1950s were losing with magnificence and stolid grace but to Shibe Park in Philadelphia, house of the Athletics and Phillies, where on a Tuesday afternoon a desultory crowd of four thousand might be present to watch senile managers fall asleep in the dugout or hapless rookies fail once again to hit the rising curve. He cannot, in short, recapture the Winners, but only the Losers: the campaign speeches of Estes Kefauver, recordings by the Bell Sisters and Guy Mitchell, the rambling confessions of minor actors before the McCarthy screening committee that they once were Communists and would appreciate the opportunity to get before the full committee and press to make a more definite statement.

Jack is infuriated by this and no wonder; he is the custodian of a unique and possibly highly marketable talent – people increasingly love the past, and a guided tour through it as opposed to records, tapes, rambling reminiscences would be enormously exciting to them – but he cannot for the life of him get to what he calls the Real Stuff, the more commercial and lovable aspects of that cuddly decade. Every time that he thinks he has recaptured Yankee Stadium in his mind and sweeps back in time to revisit it, he finds himself at Wrigley Field in Chicago where Wayne Terwilliger, now playing first base, misses a foul pop and runs straight into the stands. What can he do? What can he do about this reckless and uncontrollable talent of his, which in its sheerest perversity simply will not remit to his commands. (It is a subconscious ability, you see; if he becomes self-conscious, it leaves him entirely.) Jack is enraged. He has cold sweats, flashes of gloom and hysteria. (I forgot to say that he is a failed advertising copy writer, now working in Cleveland on display advertising mostly for the Shaker Heights district. He needs money and approbation. His marriage, his *second* marriage, is falling apart. All of this will give the plot substance and humanity, to say nothing of warm twitches of insight.) He *knows* that he is onto something big, and yet his clownish talent, all big feet and wide ears, mocks him.

He takes his problem to a psychiatrist. The psychiatrist takes some convincing, but after being taken into the offices of *Cosmos* science fiction to see the editor rejecting submissions at a penny a word, he believes everything. He says he will help Jack. This psychiatrist, who I will call Dr Mandleman, fires all of his patients and enters into a campaign to help Jack recover the more popular and marketable aspects of the fifties. He too sees the Big Money. He moves in with Jack. Together they go over the top forty charts of that era, call up retired members of the New York football Giants, pore through old Congressional Records in which McCarthy is again and again thunderously denounced by two liberal representatives. . .

Do you see the possibilities? I envision this as being somewhere around 1500 words but could expand or contract it to whatever you desire. I am very busy as always but could make room in my schedule for this project, particularly if you could see fit to give a small down payment. Would fifty dollars seem excessive? I look forward to word from you.

Dear Mr Malzberg:

I believe that you have utterly misunderstood my letter and the nature of the assignment piece.

There is nothing *funny* in a fantasy about a man who can recapture only the ugly or forgotten elements of the past. Rather, this is a bitter satire on the present which you have projected, based upon your statement that 'people love their past', with the implication that they find the future intolerable. What is funny about *that?* What is funny about failure, too? What is funny about the Philadelphia Athletics of the early 1950s with their ninety-four-year-old manager? Rather, you seem to be on the way to constructing another of your horrid metaphors for present and future, incompetence presided over by senescence.

This idea will absolutely not work, not at least within the context of a delightful comedic premise, and as you know, we are well-inventoried with work by you and others which will depress people. I cannot and will not pay fifty dollars in front for depressing stuff like this.

Perhaps you will want to take another shot at this.

Dear Editor:

Thanks for your letter. I am truly sorry that you fail to see the humour in failure or in the forgettable aspects of the past – people, I think, must learn to laugh at their foibles – but I bow to your judgment.

Might I suggest another idea which has been in mind for some time? I would like to write a story of a telepath, let me call him John, who is able to establish direct psionic links with the minds, if one can call them 'minds', of the thoroughbreds running every afternoon (except for Sundays and three months a year) at Aqueduct and Belmont race tracks in Queens, New York. John's psionic faculties work at a range of fifty yards; he is able to press his nose against the wire gate separating paddock from customers and actually get *inside* the minds of the horses. Dim thoughts like little shoots of grass press upon his own brain; he is able to determine the mental state and mood of the horses as in turn they parade by him. (Horses of course do not verbalize; John must deduce those moods subverbally.)

Obviously John is up to something. He is a mind reader; he should, through the use of this talent, be able to get some line on the outcome of a race by knowing which horses feel well, which horses' thoughts are clouded by the possibility of soporifics, which other horses' minds show vast energy because of the probable induction of stimulants. Surely he should be able to narrow the field down to two or three horses anyway which *feel good* and, by spreading his bets around these in proportion to the odds, assure himself of a good living.

(I should have said somewhat earlier on, but, as you know, am very weak at formal outlines, that John's talents are restricted to the reading of the minds of *animals*; he cannot for the life of him screen the thoughts of a fellow human. If he could, of course, he would simply check out the trainers and jockeys, but it is a perverse and limited talent, and John must make the best of what God has given him, as must we all – for instance, I outline poorly.)

The trouble is that John finds there to be no true correlation between the prerace mood or thoughts of horses and the eventual outcome. Horses that feel *well* do not necessarily win, and those horses from whom John has picked up the most depressing and suicidal emanations have been known to win. It is not a simple reversal; if it were, John would be able to make his bets on the basis of reverse correlation and do quite well this way; rather, what it seems to be is entirely *random*. Like so much of life, the prerace meditations of horses appear to have no relationship to the outcome; rather, motives and consequences are fractured, split, entirely torn apart; and this insight, which finally comes upon John after the seventh race at Aqueduct on June 12, 1974, when he has lost fifty-five dollars drives him quite mad; his soul is split, his mind shattered; he runs frantically through the sparse crowds (it is a Tuesday, and you know what OTB has done to race track attendance anyway) shouting, screaming, bellowing his rage to the heavens. 'There's no connection!' he will scream. 'Nothing makes sense, nothing connects, there is no reason at all!' and several burly Pinkertons, made sullen by rules, which require them to wear jackets and ties at all times, even on this first hot day of the year, seize him quite roughly and drag him into the monstrous computer room housing the equipment of the American Totalisor Company; there a sinister track executive, his eyes glowing with cunning and evil will say, 'Why don't you guys ever learn?' (he is a metaphor for the Devil, you see; I assure you that this will be properly planted, and the story itself will be an *allegory*) and, coming close to John, will raise a hand shaped like a talon, he will bring it upon John, he will . . .

I propose this story to be 25,000 words in length, a cover story in fact. (You and Ronald Walotsky will see the possibilities here, and Walotsky, I assure you, draws horses very well.) Although I am quite busy, the successful author of fifteen stories in this field, two of the novels published in *hardcover*, I could make time in my increasingly heavy schedule to get the story to you within twelve hours of your letter signifying outline approval. I think that an advance in this case of fifty dollars would be quite reasonable and look forward to hearing from you by return mail, holding off in the meantime from plunging into my next series of novels which, of course, are already under lucrative contract.

Dear Mr Malzberg:

We're not getting anywhere.

What in God's name is *funny* about a man who perceives 'motives and consequences to be entirely fractured . . . torn apart?' Our readers, let me assure you, have enough troubles of their own; they are already quite aware of this or do not *want* to be aware of it. Our readers, an intelligent and literate group of people numbering into the multiple thousands, have long since understood that life is unfair and inequitable, and they are looking for entertainment, release, a little bit of *joy*.

Don't you understand that this commission was for a *funny* story? There is nothing funny about your proposal, nor do I see particular humour in an allegory which will make use of the appearance of the Devil.

Perhaps we should forget this whole thing. There are other writers I would rather have approached, and it was only at the insistence of your friends that I decided to give you a chance at this one. We are heavily inventoried, as I have already said, on the despairing stuff, but if in due course you would like to send me one of your characteristic stories, *on a purely speculative basis*, I will consider it as a routine submission.

Dear Editor:

Please wait a minute or just a few minutes until you give me another chance to explain myself. I was sure that the two story ideas you have rejected, particularly the second, were quite funny; but editorial taste, as we professional writers know, is the prerogative of the editor; and if you *don't* see the humour, I can't show it to you, humour being a very rare and special thing. I am however momentarily between novels, waiting for the advance on the series contract to come through and *would* be able to write you a story at this time; let me propose one final idea to you before you come to the wrong conclusion that I am not a funny writer and go elsewhere, to some wretched hack who does not have one quarter of the bubbling humour and winsomely comprehensive view of the foibles of the human condition that I do.

I would like to write a story about a science-fiction writer, a highly successful science-fiction writer but one who nevertheless, because of certain limitations in the field and slow payment from editors, is forced to make do on an income of three thousand four hundred and eighty-three dollars a year (last year) from all of his writings and, despite the pride and delight of knowing that he is near or at the top of his field, finds getting along on such an income, particularly in the presence of a wife and family, rather difficult, his wife not understanding entirely (as she *should* understand) that science fiction is not an ultimately lucrative field for most of us but repays in satisfaction, in *great* satisfactions. This writer, who we shall call Barry, is possessed after a while by his fantasies; the partitions, in his case, between reality and fantasy have been sheared through by turmoil and economic stress, and he believes himself in many ways to be not only the creator but the receptacle of his ideas, ideas which possess him and stalk him through the night.

Barry is a gentle man, a man with a gracious sense of humour, a certain *je ne sais quoi* about him which makes him much celebrated at parties, a man whose occasionally sinister fictions serve only to mask his gay and joyous nature . . . but Barry is seized by his fantasies; people do not truly understand him, and now at last those aforementioned walls have crumpled: he takes himself to be not only the inventor but the *hero* of his plot ideas. Now he is in a capsule set on Venus flyby looking out at the green planet while he strokes his diminutive genitals and thinks of home; now again he is an archetypical alien, far from home, trying to make convincing contact with humanity; now yet again he is a rocketship, an actual physical rocketship, a phallic object extended to great length and power, zooming through the heavens, penetrating the sky.

I'll do this at 1500 words for five dollars down. Please let me hear from you.

Dear Mr Malzberg:
This was a doomed idea from the start. I hope you won't take this personally, but you need help.

Dear Editor:
My husband is at Aqueduct today, living in a motel by night, and says that he will be out of touch for at least a week, but I know he would have wanted me to acknowledge your letter,

and as soon as he returns I assume he'll be in touch with you.

I assume also that in saying that he needs 'help' you are referring to the fact that, as he told me, you were commissioning a story from him with money in front, and I hope that you can send us a cheque as soon as possible, without waiting his return. He said something about a hundred or a thousand dollars, but we'll take fifty.

Joyce Malzberg

Trolls
Robert Borski

Grady said, 'You watch out for trolls now. Hear?'

I nodded politely, slightly. 'Sure, Grady, sure. You know me.' Even so: I meant to get me one of those mothers. Maybe two.

'I'm not kidding, Harrison. You better be careful.'

'Yeah, yeah. Okay already, I'll be careful. Just quit your bitching.' Sometimes Grady gets like that: all stubborn in the head and authoritative. We have to humour him, then. Otherwise, he goes crazy. 'I'm just going out for some fresh air. Be back in an hour or so.'

I think he might have mumbled something into his beard, but I didn't hear him, because I was leaving, dispeeding. Out I went. The back door, across the lot, and into the garage. Heap was waiting for me.

(Now here's ten feet of jaguar steel with burnished chrome fenders and a hunched glass back: and it was all mine.)

I finished walking in. 'Hello, old buddy,' I says to Heap. 'How you been and all?'

No answer, of course. Heap seldom answers, so right away I ask, 'You ready for some troll-hunting?'

Heap gives smile-grin up in grillwork. That means *yes* in car.

'Okay baby,' I said climbing in, 'let's go get 'em.'

I turned the key and Heap fired up from inside, lizard-gut burning acid. Eyes opened, and glare lights phased out hungrily. I found the wheel and massaged Heap's metal brain with the foot pedals. Smelled troll blood already, felt so good.

We were gonna get one, maybe two. So I coaxed Heap out onto the street, tail end hot hot hot.

It was July. Good troll-hunting weather. Summer nights like these usually brought them out in droves (making up perhaps for those troll-less winters). I knew we had a good chance of catching one, although two would bring our average up.

Like altogether now, I guess me and Heap had killed on up to thirty-six trolls. (That's no brag, either, only telling facts.) Match that against three years' driving experience and you get an average of one troll a month. Not bad, eh?

Course me and Heap were nowheres near establishing a record. Not when some Johnny down in Phoenix was putting them away six, seven a month. But we might make the ratings someday and that was good enough for us KayCee folk.

Right, Heap?

Anyways, see, we were on concrete now, on the inroads of the Intercity. Snakebelly smooth as far as the eye could see, miles and miles of highway with only slapdash yellow signs marking the exits and entrances: old Intercity 16. It was our favourite road and we were happy to be back on familiar territory.

Seems funny when you think about it, though. That back when Grady was my age –

Case I forgot to mention it, Grady's my stepfather on my brother's side. The guy who was always warning me to look out for trolls (he worried about me so).

– none of this was here. They had greens and scenes instead. Trunks with trees, and grass, rockribs and weeds.

I guess there were a lot of ecology-minded hicks around in those days.

But nowadays, in 1994, it's different. We're more into the concrete revolution. Cities have become our lifeblood, the roads our arteries. So now you can't escape them. They're ubiquitous. Everywhere you go, everyplace you see: concrete. In greystone blocks or flatbed lamina.

Just beautiful.

With all our food being produced synthetically or in hydroponic centres, what's the use of having countryside anyway?

No use. That's why we got rid of it, got concretized. Made more sense, wouldn't you say?

And in a way, all this pavement was responsible for the surfacing of trolls. With their type of country – the picnic-type – being slowly wiped out, they had nowhere else to go.

You could almost say they were like jackrabbits.

Back when God's country was underdeveloped and raw, there were droves and droves of jackrabbits hunkering up and down the countryside. Yet very few people ever noticed them. But then when they started building transcontinental highways and expressways, these rabbits started getting pushed out of their own territory. They had to start crossing concrete to get anywhere, and that's when people started noticing them; when they were scurrying across the road or getting trammelled under the wheels, crunch crunch.

Well, trolls were sort of the same way.

They were limited in the places they could make the nature scene. A few oases here and there. A stretch of grass and weeds up near the riverside. But that's about all. And in every case, these places were surrounded with concrete.

(But now, you see, this doesn't mean anything unless you realize several things. Like the fact that trolls are masters of disguise. They look exactly like you or me or Joe Bob next door. Only thing is, they're hicks at heart. That's right, hicks. They miss the greenery and the growing things. The cutfresh smell of grass, the scratchquick scurry of leaves. That's why they ramble about so: they're looking for some place to flake out on. Someplace green, like oases or along the Missouri River. To get there, though, they have to park their cars nearby, and cut across the remaining concrete on foot. Which is illegal. Which is where me and Heap come in. We try and juice 'em before they can make it to where they're headed. Or if we miss them first time around, we try again when the trolls have to leave by the same way they came.

Troll-hunting: that's how it's done and what it's all about. I hope you paid attention, friend.

All right. We were on snakebelly smooth again, old Intercity 16. Everything was going fine. Heap was burning ass, my eyes were eaglesharp, on the lookout. Weather, too, was good. Up above, at least as far above as the upper limits of Heap's hunched glass back, the sky was clear, with fixated stars. Temperaturewise, the air was citywarm and muggy. All of which was great. There were bound to be trolls out tonight.

Heap squealed his wheels in anticipation, drawing my adrenalin to the surface. Another three to four miles, and we would be in troll country. I started to watch the outer lanes for parked cars.

Last time me and Heap were out here, about three weeks ago, we bagged a starry-eyed grandma troll. She was walking along the road with a fistfull of green when we came around the bend and juiced her. *Splot!* All over the road and half over the car. Took me two weeks just to pick her out of Heap's grillwork.

But the satisfaction of it all. What can I say? Every time me and Heap wiped out a troll, my spine felt like it had been short-circuited, like electrocuted fudge. That, plus knowing we were probably gonna make the ratings someday made everything worth any trouble involved. And that included cleaning up Heap's grillwork.

So you really can't blame me for being the way I was. It was in my blood. Heap's too. We were born troll killers.

Which brings us back to tonight, and those old familiar riffs about how we were gonna get one, maybe two. Because now we were there, in troll country.

I slowed down, turning the infra-red darksight system on. Heap was purring beneath me like a contented cyclotron. It was dangerous, driving this way, though, so we kept our eyes peeled. Didn't want to run into a shadowload of parked car. In fact –

. . . hey, wait a minute. I thought I saw something . . .

Yes, there it was. Just what we were looking for. A parked car, up ahead to the left. That meant there was a troll somewheres around here. (There were also no other cars in sight. Which meant the troll was ours. Good. Good.)

All excited like, I felt my temples start to pound. I was breathing heavier, too, like I was about to reach orgasm. My palms were sweaty. I doubt if I blinked once.

We cruised up the road a smooth forty-five, taking it easy. And then I saw him: the troll. He was running left-to-right, some 75 yards away, all at a zigzag. Immediately, I unmasked Heap, hoping the lights would blind him. They didn't, though, 65 I guess because our manoeuvre wasn't all that unexpected 60 (this troll had obviously been around for a while). But he was a goner just the same 50. His car was to our rear, and the nearest 45 embankment was a hundred yards past the perpendicular line running up from his shoulder blades 39 and he certainly wasn't about to turn back now. In fact, his only chance was to face us head on 25 and try to dodge us like a matador 20 would a bull. Which wasn't going to be easy 15 because me and Heap were experts at this sort of thing 10 having done it countless times before 9 and never having lost one yet 8. We were closer now. I could see him 7 dancing in the light. But what was that 6 in his hand? 5 Flowers? And why did 4 he suddenly 3 look so familiar 2 as he feigned right, but instead 1 went left, which 0 –

I heard the muted thud of impact.

– is where we hit him, crash slam.

Several things happened at once, then. Out of the corners of my eyes, I saw the troll's shattered body bounce silently down the road, like something out of a speeded-up soundless movie, all bloodied and broken, while up in my head, in my mind's eye, I was replaying the last few seconds before impact.

Backwards from ten: there was that funny little troll running with short, tired strides, his arms swinging back-forth, his beard lightning yellow in the lights. There was Heap and me nosing in on him, relentlessly, doggingly, like some archfiend out of the pulp tradition (me and Heap were weaned on Capt. Whizzflash). Next there was a silence, the sky dark with frozen salt and shadows; then there was the collision at zero, and the recognition. The fire inside, the acid belly broth. Then there was no more Grady, cause he was a troll, and me and Heap had just zonked him for number thirty-seven.

You can understand how shocked we were.

But it was like I told you: trolls were tricky sons of bitches. They could be almost anyone, maybe even you reading this or Joe Bob next door. And it makes no difference who you are, cause like Grady and me and Heap were real close, and the best of buddies and all, but as it turned out, he was troll and he had to go, you know.

So take warning, you trolls hereabout. Otherwise, we'll get you no matter how much it hurts hurts hurts.

Right, Heap?

Elephant With Wooden Leg
John Sladek

Note: Madmen are often unable to distinguish between dream, reality, and . . . between dream and reality. None of the incidents in Henry LaFarge's narrative ever happened or could have happened. His 'Orinoco Institute' bears no relation to the actual think tank of that name, his 'Drew Blenheim' in no way resembles the famous futurologist, and his 'United States of America' is not even a burlesque upon the real United States of Armorica.

I couldn't hear him.

'Can't hear you, Blenheim. The line must be bad.'

'Or mad, Hank. I wonder what that would take?'

'What what?'

'What would it take to drive a telephone system out of its mind, eh? So that it wasn't just giving wrong numbers, but madly right ones. Let's see: Content-addressable computer memories to shift the conversations . . .'

I stopped listening. A bug was crawling up the window frame across the room. It moved like a cockroach, but I couldn't be sure.

'Look, Blenheim, I'm pretty busy today. Is there something on your mind?'

He ploughed right on. ' . . . so if you're trying to reserve a seat on the plane to Seville, you'd get a seat at the opera instead. While the person who wants the opera seat is really making an appointment with a barber, whose customer is just then talking to the box-office of *Hair*, or maybe making a hairline reservation . . .'

'Blenheim, I'm talking to you.'

'Yes?'

'What was it you called me up about?'

'Oh, this and that. I was wondering, for instance, whether parrots have internal clocks.'

'What?' I still couldn't be sure whether the bug was a cockroach or not, but I saluted just in case.

'If so, maybe we could get them to act as speaking clocks.'

He sounded crazier than ever. What trivial projects for one of the best brains in our century – no wonder he was on leave.

'Blenheim, I'm busy. Institute work must go on, you know.'

'Yes. Tell you what, why don't you drop over this afternoon? I have something to talk over with you.'

'Can't. I have a meeting all afternoon.'

'Fine, fine. See you, then. Anytime around 4:43.'

Madmen never listen.

Helmut Rasmussen came in just as Blenheim hung up. He seemed distressed. Not that his face showed it; ever since that bomb wrecked his office, Hel has been unable to move his face. Hysterical paralysis, Dr Grobe had explained.

But Hel could signal whatever he felt by fiddling with the stuff in his shirt pocket. For anger, his red pencil came out (and sometimes underwent a savage sharpening), impatience made him work his slide rule, surprise made him glance into his pocket diary, and so on.

Just now he was clicking the button on his ballpoint pen with some agitation. For a moment he actually seemed about to take it out and draw worry lines on his forehead.

'What is it, Hel? The costing on Project Faith?' He spread the schedules on my desk and pointed to the snag: a discrepancy between the estimated cost of blasting apart and hauling away the Rocky Mountains, and the value of oil recovered in the process.

'I see. The trains, eh? Diesels seem to use most of the oil we get. How about steam locomotives, then?'

He clapped me on the shoulder and nodded.

'By the way, Hel, I won't be at the meeting today. Blenheim just called up. Wants to see me.'

Hel indicated surprise.

'Look, I know he's a crackpot. You don't have to pocket-diary me, I know he's nuts. But he is also technically still the Director. Our boss. They haven't taken him off the payroll, just put him on sick leave. Besides, he used to have a lot of good ideas.'

Hel took out a felt-tip pen and began to doodle with some sarcasm. The fact was, Blenheim had completely lost his grip during his last year at the Institute. Before the government forced him to take leave, he'd been spending half a million a year on developing, rumours said, glass pancakes. And who could forget his plan to arm police with chocolate revolvers?

'Sure he's had a bad time, but maybe he's better now,' I said, without conviction.

Institute people never get better, Hel seemed to retort. They just kept on making bigger and better decisions, with more and more brilliance and finality, until they broke. Like glass pancakes giving out an ever purer ring, they exploded.

It was true. Like everyone else here, I was seeing Dr Grobe, our resident psychiatrist, several times a week. Then there were cases beyond even the skiil of Dr Grobe: Joe Feeney, who interrupted his work (on the uses of holograms) one day to announce that he was a filing cabinet. Edna Bessler, who believed that she was being pursued by a synthetic *a priori* proposition. The lovely entomologist Pawlie Sutton, who disappeared. And George Hoad, whose rocket research terminated when he walked into the Gents one day and cut his throat. George spent the last few minutes of consciousness vainly trying to mop up the bloody floor with toilet paper . . .

Something was wrong with the personnel around this place, all right. And I suspected that our little six-legged masters knew more about this than they were saying.

Finally I mumbled, 'I know it's useless, Hel. But I'd better find out what he wants.'

You do what you think is best, Hel thought. He stalked out of my office then, examining the point on his red pencil.

The bug was a cockroach, *P. americana*. It sauntered across the wall until it reached the curly edge of a wall poster, then it flew about a foot to land on the nearest dark spot. This was Uncle Sam's right eye. Uncle Sam, with his accusing eyes and finger, was trying to recruit men for the Senate and House of Representatives. On this poster, he said, 'The Senate Needs MEN'. So far, the recruitment campaign was a failure. Who could blame people for not wanting to go on the 'firing line' in Washington? The casualty rate of Congressmen was 30 per cent annually, and climbing, in spite of every security measure we could think of.

Which reminded me of work. I scrubbed off the blackboard and started laying out a contingency tree for Project Pogo, a plan to make the whole cabinet – all one hundred and forty-three secretaries – completely mobile, hence, proof against revolution. So far the Security Secretary didn't care for the idea of 'taking to our heels', but it was cheaper to keep the cabinet on the move than to guard them in Washington.

The cockroach, observing my industry, left by a wall ventilator, and I breathed easier. The contingency tree didn't look so interesting by now, and out the window I could see real trees.

The lawn rolled away down from the building to the river (not the Orinoco, despite our name). The far bank was blue-black with pines, and the three red maples on our lawn, this time of year, stood out like three separate, brilliant fireballs. For just the duration of a bluejay's flight from one to another, I could forget about the stale routine, the smell of chalkdust.

I remembered a silly day three years ago, when I'd carved a heart on one of those trees, with Pawlie Sutton's initials and my own.

Now a security guard strolled his puma into view. They stopped under the nearest maple and he snapped the animal's lead. It was up the trunk in two bounds, and out of sight among the leaves. While that stupid-faced man in uniform looked up, the fireball shook and swayed above him. A few great leaves fell, bright as drops of blood.

Now what was *this* headache going to be about?

All the big problems were solved, or at least we knew how to solve them. The world was just about the way we wanted it, now, except we no longer seemed to want it that way. That's how Mr Howell, the Secretary of Personal Relationships, had put it in his telecast. What was missing? God, I think he said. God had made it possible for us to dam the Amazon and move the Orinoco, to feed India and dig gold from the ocean floor and cure cancer. And now God – the way he said it made you feel that He, too, was in the Cabinet – God was going to help us get down and solve our personal, human problems. Man's inhumanity to man. The lack of communication. The hatred. God and Secretary Howell were going to get right down to some committee work on this. I think that was the telecast where Howell announced the introduction of detention camps for 'malcontents'. Just until we got our personal problems all ironed out. I had drawn up the plans for these camps that summer. Then George Hoad borrowed my pocket-knife one day and never gave it back. Then the headaches started.

As I stepped outside, the stupid-faced guard was looking up the skirt of another tree.

'Prrt, prrt,' he said quietly, and the black puma dropped to earth beside him. There was something hanging out of its mouth that looked like a bluejay's wing.

'Good girl. Good girl.'

I hurried away to the helicopter.

Drew Blenheim's tumbledown mansion sits in the middle

of withered woods. For half a mile around, the trees are laced together with high-voltage fence. Visitors are blindfolded and brought in by helicopter. There are also rumours of minefields and other security measures. At that time, I put it all down to Blenheim's paranoia.

The engine shut down with the sound of a coin spinning to rest. Hands helped me out and removed my blindfold. The first thing I saw, hanging on a nearby stretch of fence, was a lump of bones and burnt fur from some small animal. The guards and their submachine-guns escorted me only as far as the door, for Blenheim evidently hated seeing signs of the security he craved. The house looked dismal and decayed – the skull of some dead Orinoco Institute?

A servant wearing burnt cork makeup and white gloves ushered me through a dim hallway that smelled of hay and on into the library.

'I'll tell Mr Blenheim you're here, sir. Perhaps you'd care to read one of his monographs while you wait?'

I flicked through *The Garden of Regularity* (a slight tract recommending that older people preserve intestinal health by devouring their own dentures) and opened an insanely boring book called *Can Bacteria Read?* I was staring uncomprehendingly at one of its pages when a voice said:

'Are you still here?' The plump old woman had evidently been sitting in her deep chair when I came in. As she craned around at me, I saw she had a black eye. Something was wrong with her hair, too. 'I thought you'd left by now – oh, it's *you*.'

'Madam, do I know you?'

She sat forward and put her face to the light. The black eye was tattooed, and the marcelled hair was really a cap of paper, covered with wavy ink lines. But it was Edna Bessler, terribly aged.

'You've changed, Edna.'

'So would you, young man, if you'd been chased around a nuthouse for two years by a synthetic *a priori* proposition.'

She sniffed. 'Well, thank heavens the revolution is set for tomorrow.'

I laughed nervously. 'Well, Edna, it certainly is good to see you. What are you doing here, anyway?'

'There are quite a few of the old gang here, Joe Feeney and – and others. This place has become a kind of repair depot for mad futurologists. Blenheim is very kind, but of course he's quite mad himself. Mad as a wet hen. As you see from his writing.'

'*Can Bacteria Read?* I couldn't read it.'

'Oh, he thinks that germs are, like people, amenable to suggestion. So, with the proper application of mass hypnosis among the microbe populations, we ought to be able to cure any illness with any quack remedy.'

I nodded. 'Hope he recovers soon. I'd like to see him back at the Institute, working on real projects again. Big stuff, like the old days. I'll never forget the old Drew Blenheim, the man who invented satellite dialling.'

Satellite dialling came about when the malcontents were trying to jam government communications systems, cut lines and blow up exchanges. Blenheim's system virtually made each telephone a complete exchange in itself, dialling directly through a satellite. Voice signals were compressed and burped skywards in short bursts that evaded most jamming signals. It was an Orinoco Institute triumph over anarchy.

Edna chuckled. 'Oh, he's working on real projects. I said he was mad, not useless. Now if you'll help me out of this chair, I must go fix an elephant.'

I was sure I'd misheard this last. After she'd gone, I looked over a curious apparatus in the corner. Parts of it were recognizable – a clock inside a parrot cage, a gas laser, and a fringed shawl suspended like a flag from a walking-stick thrust into a watermelon – but their combination was baffling.

At 4:43 by the clock in the cage, the blackface servant took me to a gloomy great hall place, scattered with the shapes of easy chairs and sofas. A figure in a diving suit rose from the piano and waved me to a chair. Then it sat down again, flipping out its airhoses behind the bench.

For a few minutes I suffered through a fumbling version of some Mexican tune. But when Blenheim – no doubt it was he – stood up and started juggling oranges, I felt it was time to speak out.

'Look, I've interrupted my work to come here. Is this all you have to show me?'

One of the oranges vaulted high, out of sight in the gloom above; another hit me in the chest. The figure opened its face-plate and grinned. 'Long time no see, Hank.'

It was me.

'Rubber mask,' Blenheim explained, plucking at it. 'I couldn't resist trying it on you, life gets so tedious here. Ring for Rastus, will you? I want to shed this suit.'

We made small talk while the servant helped him out of the heavy diving suit. Rather, Blenheim rattled on alone; I wasn't feeling well at all. The shock of seeing myself had reminded me of something I should remember, but couldn't.

'. . . to build a heraldry vending machine. Put in a coin, punch out your name, and it prints a coat-of-arms. Should suit those malcontents, eh? All they probably really want is a coat-of-arms.'

'They're just plain evil,' I said. 'When I think how they bombed poor Hel Rasmussen's office – '

'Oh, he did that himself. Didn't you know?'

'Suicide? So that explains the hysterical paralysis!'

My face looked exasperated, as Blenheim peeled it off. 'Is that what Dr Grobe told you? Paralysed hell, the blast blew his face clean off. Poor Hel's present face is a solid plate of plastic, bolted on. He breathes through a hole in his shoulder and feeds himself at the armpit. If Grobe told you any different, he's just working on your morale.'

From upstairs came a kind of machine-gun clatter. The minstrel servant glided in with a tray of drinks.

'Oh, Rastus. Tell the twins not to practice their tap-dancing just now, will you? Hank looks as if he has a headache.'

'Yes sir. By the way, the three-legged elephant has arrived. I put it in the front hall. I'm afraid the prosthesis doesn't fit.'

'I'll fix it. Just ask Jumbo to lean up against the wall for half an hour.'

'Very good, sir.'

After this, I decided to make my escape from this Bedlam.

'Doesn't anybody around here ever do anything straight-forward or say anything in plain English?'

'We're trying to tell you something, Hank, but it isn't easy. For one thing, I'm not sure we can trust you.'

'Trust me for what?'

His twisted face twisted out a smile. 'If you don't know, then how can we trust you? But come with me to the con-servatory and I'll show you something.'

We went to a large room with dirty glass walls. To me it looked like nothing so much as a bombed-out workshop. Though there were bags of fertilizer on the floor, there wasn't a living plant in sight. Instead, the tables were littered with machinery and lab equipment: jumbles of retorts and coloured wires and nuts and bolts that made no sense.

'What do you see, Hank?'

'Madness and chaos. You might as well have pears in the light sockets and a banana on the telephone cradle, for all I can make of it.'

He laughed. 'That's better. We'll crazify you yet.'

I pointed to a poster-covered cylinder standing in the corner. One of the posters had Uncle Sam, saying 'I Need MEN for Congress'.

'What's that Parisian advertising kiosk doing here?'

'Rastus built that for us, out of scrap alloys I had lying around. Like it?'

I shrugged. 'The top's too pointed. It looks like – '

'Yes, go on.'

'This is silly. All of you need a few sessions with Dr Grobe,' I said. 'I'm leaving.'

'I was afraid you'd say that. But it's you who need another session with Dr Grobe, Hank.'

'You think *I'm* crazy?'

'No, you're too damned sane.'

'Well you sure as hell are nuts!' I shouted. 'Why bother with all the security outside? Afraid someone will steal the idea of a minstrel show or the secret of a kiosk?'

He laughed again. 'Hank, those guards aren't there to keep strangers out. *They're to keep us in.* You see, my house really and truly is a madhouse.'

I stamped out a side door and ordered my helicopter.

'My head's killing me,' I told the guard. 'Take it easy with that blindfold.'

'Oh, sorry, mac. Hey look, it's none of my business, but what did you do with that tree you brung with you?'

'Tree?' God, even the guards were catching it.

That evening I went to see Dr Grobe.

'Another patient? I swear, I'm going to install a revolving door on this office. Sit down. Uh, Hank LaFarge, isn't it? Sit down, Hank. Let's see . . . oh, you're the guy who's afraid of cockroaches, right?'

'Not exactly afraid of them. In fact they remind me of someone I used to be fond of. Pawlie Sutton used to work with them. But my problem is, I know that cockroaches are the real bosses. We're just kidding ourselves with our puppet government, our Uncle Sham – '

He chuckled appreciatively.

'But what "bugs" me is, nobody will recognize this plain and simple truth, Doctor.'

'Ah, ah. Remember last time, you agreed to call me by my first name.'

'Sorry, uh, Oddpork.' I couldn't imagine why anyone with that name wanted to be called by it, unless the doctor himself was trying to get used to it. He was an odd-pork of a man, too: plump and rumpy, with over-large hands that never stopped adjusting his already well-adjusted clothes. He always looked surprised at everything I said, even 'hello'. Every session, he made the same joke about the revolving door.

Still, repetitive jokes help build a family atmosphere, which was probably what he wanted. There was a certain comfort in this stale atmosphere of no surprises. Happy families are all alike, and their past is exactly like their future.

'Hank, I haven't asked you directly about your cockroach theory before, have I? Want to tell me about it?'

'I know it sounds crazy at first. For one thing, cockroaches aren't very smart, I know that. In some ways, they're stupider than ants. And their communication equipment isn't much, either. Touch and smell, mainly. They aren't naturally equipped for conquering the world.'

Oddpork lit a cigar and leaned back, looking at the ceiling 'What do they do with the world when they get it?'

'That's another problem. After all, they don't *need* the world. All they need is food, water, a fair amount of darkness and some warmth. But there's the key, you see?

'I mean we humans have provided for all these needs for many centuries. Haphazardly, though. So it stands to reason that life would be better for them if we worked for them on a regular basis. But to get us to do that, they have to take over first.'

He tried to blow a smoke ring, failed, and adjusted his tie. 'Go on. How do they manage this takeover?'

'I'm not sure, but I think they have help. Maybe some smart tinkerer wanted to see what would happen if he gave them good long-distance vision. Maybe he was so pleased with the result that he then taught them to make semaphore signals with their feelers. The rest is history.'

Dusting his lapel, Dr Grobe said, 'I don't quite follow. Semaphore signals?'

'One cockroach is stupid. But a few thousand of them in

good communication could make up a fair brain. Our tinkerer probably hastened that along by intensive breeding and group learning problems, killing off the failures . . . it would take ten years at the outside.'

'Really? And how long would the conquest of man take? How would the little insects fare against the armies of the world?'

'They never need to try. Armies are run by governments, and governments are run, for all practical purposes, by small panels of experts. Think tanks like the Orinoco Institute. And – this just occurred to me – for all practical purposes, you run the Institute.'

For once, Dr Grobe did not look surprised. 'Oh, so I'm in on the plot, am I?'

'We're all so crazy, we really depend on you. You can ensure that we work for the good of the cockroaches, or else you can get rid of us – send us away, or encourage our suicides.'

'Why should I do that?'

'Because *you* are afraid of them.'

'Not at all.' But his hand twitched, and a little cigar ash fell on his immaculate trousers. I felt my point was proved.

'Damn. I'll have to sponge that. Excuse me.'

He stepped into his private washroom and closed the door. My feeling of triumph suddenly faded. Maybe I was finally cracking. What evidence did I really have?

On the other hand, Dr Grobe was taking a long time in there. I stole over to the washroom door and listened.

'. . . verge of suicide . . . ,' he murmured. '. . . yes . . give up the idea, but . . . yes, that's just what I . . .'

I threw back the door on a traditional spy scene. In the half-darkness, Dr G was hunched over the medicine cabinet, speaking into a microphone. He wore earphones.

'Hank, don't be a foo – '

I hit him, not hard, and he sat down on the edge of the tub. He looked resigned.

'So this is my imagined conspiracy, is it? Where do these wires lead?'

They led inside the medicine cabinet, to a tiny apparatus. A dozen brown ellipses had clustered around it, like a family around the TV.

'Let me explain,' he said.

'Explanations are unnecessary, Doctor. I just want to get out of here, unless your six-legged friends can stop me.'

'They might. So could I. I could order the guards to shoot you. I could have you put away with your crazy friends. I could even have you tried for murder, just now.'

'Murder?' I followed his gaze back into the office. From under the desk, a pair of feet. 'Who's that?'

'Hel Rasmussen. Poisoned himself a few minutes before you came in. Believe me, it wasn't pleasant, seeing the poor fellow holding a bottle of cynanide to his armpit. He left a note blaming you, in a way.'

'Me!'

'You were the last straw. This afternoon, he saw you take an axe and deliberately cut down one of those beautiful maple trees in the yard. Destruction of beauty – it was too much for him.'

Trees again. I went to the office window and looked out at the floodlit landscape. One of the maples was missing.

Dr Grobe and I sat down again at our respective interview stations, while I thought this over. Blenheim and his mask came into it, I was sure of that. But why?

Dr Grobe fished his lifeless cigar from the ashtray. 'The point is, I can stop you from making any trouble for me. So you may as well hear me out.' He scratched a match on the sole of Hel's shoe and relit the cigar.

'All right, Oddpork. You win. What happens now?'

'Nothing much. Nothing at all. If my profession has any meaning, it's to keep things from happening.' He blew out the match. 'I'm selling ordinary life. Happiness, as you must now see, lies in developing a pleasant, comfortable and productive routine – and then sticking to it. No unpleasant surprises. No shocks. Psychiatry has always aimed for that, and now it is within our grasp. The cockroach conspiracy hasn't taken over the world, but it has taken over the Institute – and it's our salvation.

'You see, Hank, our bargain isn't one-sided. We give them a little shelter, a few scraps of food. But they give us something far more important: real organization. *The life of pure routine.*'

I snorted. 'Like hurrying after trains? Or wearing ourselves out on assembly-line work? Or maybe grinding our lives away in boring offices? Punching time-clocks and marching in formation?'

'None of the above, thank you. Cockroaches never hurry to anything but dinner. They wouldn't march in formation except for fun. They are free – yet they are part of a highly organized society. And this can be ours.'

'If we're not all put in detention camps.'

'Listen, those camps are only a stage. So what if a few million grumblers get sterilized and shut away for a year or two? Think of the *billions* of happy, decent citizens, enjoying a freedom they have earned. Someday, every man will live exactly as he pleases – and his pleasure will lie in serving his fellow men.'

Put like that, it was persuasive. Another half-hour of this and I was all but convinced.

'Sleep on it, eh Hank? Let me know tomorrow what you think.' His large hand on my shoulder guided me to the door.

'You may be right,' I said, smiling back at him. I meant it, too. Even though the last thing I saw, as the door closed, was a stream of glistening brown that came from under the washroom door and disappeared under the desk.

I sat up in my own office most of the night, staring out at the maple stump. There was no way out: Either I worked for *Periplaneta americana* and gradually turned into a kind of moral cockroach myself, or I was killed. And there were certain advantages to either choice.

I was about to turn on the video-recorder to leave a suicide note, when I noticed the cassette was already recorded. I ran it back and played it.

Blenheim came on, wearing my face and my usual suit.

'They think I'm you, Hank, dictating some notes. Right now you're really at my house, reading a dull book in the library. So dull, in fact, that it's guaranteed to put you into a light trance. When I'm safely back, Edna will come in and wake you.

'She's not as loony as she seems. The black eye is inked for her telescope, and the funny cap with lines on it, that looks like marcelled hair, that's a weathermap. I won't explain why she's doing astronomy – you'll understand in time.

'On the other hand, she's got a fixation that the stars are nothing but the shiny backs of cockroaches, treading around the heavenly spheres. It makes a kind of sense when you think of it: *Periplaneta* means around the world, and America being the home of the Star-Spangled Banner.

'Speaking of national anthems, Mexico's is La Cucaracha – another cockroach reference. They seem to be taking over this message!

'The gang and I have been thinking about bugs a lot lately. Of course Pawlie has always thought about them, but the rest of us . . .' I missed the next part. So Pawlie was at the madhouse? And they hadn't told me?

'. . . when I started work on the famous glass pancakes. I discovered a peculiar feature of glass discs, such as those found on clock faces.

'Say, you can do us a favour. I'm coming around at dawn with the gang, to show you a gadget or two. We haven't got all the bugs out of them yet, but – will you go into Dr Grobe's office at dawn, and check the time on his clock? But first, smash the glass on his window, will you? Thanks. I'll compensate him for it later.

'Then go outside the building, but on no account stand

between the maple stump and the broken window. The best place to wait is on the little bluff to the North, where you'll have a good view of the demonstration. We'll meet you there.

'Right now you see our ideas darkly, as through a pancake, I guess. But soon you'll understand. You see, we're a kind of cockroach ourselves. I mean, living on scraps of sanity. We have to speak in parables and work in silly ways because *they* can't. *They* live in a comfortable kind of world where elephants have their feet cut off to make umbrella stands. We have to make good use of the three-legged elephants.

'Don't bother destroying this cassette. It won't mean a thing to any right-living insect.'

It didn't mean much to me, not yet. Cockroaches in the stars? Clocks? There were questions I had to ask, at the rendezvous.

There was one question I'd already asked that needed an answer. Pawlie had been messing about in her lab, when I asked her to marry me. Two years ago, was it? Or three?

'But you don't like cockroaches,' she said.

'No, and I'll never ask a cockroach for its claw in marriage.' I looked over her shoulder into the glass case. 'What's so interesting about these?'

'Well, for one thing, they're not laboratory animals. I caught them myself in the basement here at the Institute. See? Those roundish ones are the nymphs – sexless adolescents. Cute, aren't they?'

I had to admit they were. A little. 'They look like the fat black exclamation points in comic strips,' I observed.

'They're certainly healthy, all of them. I've never seen any like them. I – that's funny.' She went and fetched a book, and looked from some illustration to the specimens under glass.

'What's funny?'

'Look, I'm going to be dissecting the rest of the afternoon. Meet you for dinner. Bye.'

'You haven't answered my question, Pawlie.'

'Bye.'

That was the last I saw of her. Later, Dr Grobe put it about that she'd been found, hopelessly insane. Still later, George Hoad cut his throat.

The floodlights went off, and I could see dawn greyness and mist. I took a can of beans and went for a stroll outside.

One of the guards nodded a wary greeting. They and their cats were always jumpiest at this time of day.

'Everything all right, officer?'

'Yeah. Call me crazy, but I think I just heard an elephant.'

When he and his puma were out of sight, I heaved the can of beans through Dr Grobe's lighted window.

'What the hell?' he shouted. I slipped back to my office, waited a few minutes, then went to see him.

A slender ray came through the broken window and struck the clock on the opposite wall. Grobe sat transfixed, staring at it with more surprise than ever. And no wonder, for the clock had become a parrot.

'Relax, Oddpork,' I said. 'It's only some funny kind of holo-gram in the clock face, worked by a laser from the lawn. You look like a comic villain, sitting there with that cigar stub in your face.'

The cigar stub moved. Looking closer, I saw it was made up of the packed tails of a few cockroaches, trying to force them-selves between his closed lips. More ran up from his spotless collar and joined them, and others made for his nostrils. One approached the queue at the mouth, found another stuck there, and had a nibble at its kicking hind leg.

'Get away! Get away!' I gave Grobe a shake to dislodge them, and his mouth fell open. A brown flood of kicking bodies tumbled out and down, over his well-cut lapels.

I had stopped shuddering by the time I joined the others on the bluff. Pawlie and Blenheim were missing. Edna stopped scanning the horizon with her brass telescope long enough to introduce me to the pretty twins, Alice and Celia. They sat in the grass beside a tangled heap of revolvers, polishing their patent-leather tap shoes.

The unbiquitous Rastus was wiping off his burnt cork makeup. I asked him why.

'Don't need it anymore. Last night it was my camouflage. I was out in the woods, cutting a path through the electric fence. Quite a wide path, as you'll understand.'

He continued removing the black until I recognized the late George Hoad.

'George! But you cut your throat, remember? Mopping up blood – '

'Hank, that was your blood. It was you cut your throat in the Gents, after Pawlie vanished. Remember?'

I did, giddily. 'What happened to you, then?'

'Your suicide attempt helped me make up my mind; I quit the Institute next day. You were still in the hospital.'

Still giddy, I turned to watch Joe Feeney operating the curious laser I'd seen in the library. Making parrots out of clocks.

'I understand now,' I said. 'But what's the watermelon for?'

'Cheap cooling device.'

'And the "flag"?' I indicated the shawl-stick arrangement.

'To rally round. I stuck it in the melon because they were using the umbrella stand for – '

'Look!' Edna cried. 'The attack begins!' She handed me a second telescope.

All I saw below was the lone figure of Blenheim in his diving suit, shuffling slowly up from the river mist to face seven guards and two pumas. He seemed to be juggling croquet balls.

'Why don't we help him?' I shouted. 'Don't just sit here shining shoes and idling.'

The twins giggled. 'We've already helped some,' said Alice, nodding at the pile of weapons. 'We made friends with the guards.'

I got the point when those below pulled their guns on Blenheim. As each man drew, he looked at his gun and then threw it away.

'What a waste,' Celia sighed. 'Those guns are made from just about the best chocolate you can get.'

Blenheim played his parlour trick on the nearest guard: one juggled ball flew high, the guard looked up, and a second ball clipped him on the upturned chin.

Now the puma guards went into action.

'I can't look,' I said, my eye glued to the telescope. One of the animals stopped to sniff at a sticky revolver, but the other headed straight for his quarry. He leapt up, trying to fasten his claws into the stranger's big brass head.

Out of the river mist came a terrible cry, and then a terrible sight: a hobbling grey hulk that resolved into a charging elephant. Charging diagonally, so it looked even larger.

The pumas left the scene. One fled in our direction until Alice snatched up a pistol and fired it in the air. At that sound, the guards decided to look for jobs elsewhere. After all, as Pawlie said later, you couldn't expect a man to face a juggling diver *and* a mad elephant with a wooden leg, with nothing but a chocolate ·38, not on *those* wages.

Pawlie was riding on the neck of the elephant. When he came to a wobbling stop I saw that one of Jumbo's forelegs was a section of tree with the bark still on it. And in the bark, a heart with PS + HL, carved years before.

I felt the triumph was all over – especially since Pawlie kept nodding her head yes at me – until George said:

'Come on, gang. Let's set it up.'

Jumbo had been pulling a wooden sledge, bearing the Paris kiosk. Now he went off to break his fast on water and grass, while the rest of us set the thing upright. Even before we had fuelled it with whatever was in the fertilizer bags, I guessed that it was a rocket.

After some adjustments, the little door was let down, and a sweet, breakfast pancake odour came forth. Joe Feeney

opened a flask of dark liquid and poured it in the entrance.
The smell grew stronger.

'Maple sap,' he explained. 'From Jumbo's wooden leg.
Mixed with honey. And there's oatmeal inside. A farewell
breakfast.'

I looked in the little door and saw the inside of the ship was
made like a metal honeycomb, plenty of climbing room for
our masters.

Pawlie came from the building with a few cockroaches in a
jar, and let them taste our wares. Then, all at once, it was a
sale opening at any big department store. We all stood back
and let the great brown wave surge forward and break over the
little rocket. Some of them, nymphs especially, scurried all
the way up to the nose cone and back down again in their
excitement. It all looked so jolly that I tried not to think about
their previous meals.

Edna glanced at her watch. 'Ten minutes more,' she said.
'Or they'll hit the sun.'

I objected that we'd never get all of them loaded in ten
minutes.

'No,' said Pawlie, 'But we'll get the best and strongest. The
shrews can keep the rest in control.'

Edna closed the door, and the twins did a vigorous tap-dance
on the unfortunate stragglers. A few minutes later, a million
members of the finest organization on earth were on their
way to the stars.

'To join their little friends,' said Edna.

Pawlie and I touched hands, as Blenheim opened his face-
plate.

'I've been making this study,' he said, 'of spontaneous
combustion in giraffes . . .'

Planting Time
Pete Adams and
Charles Nightingale

Randy Richmond was bored, excessively, intolerably, and what felt like eternally, bored. He was so bored, in fact, that he no longer wondered what kind of programme the hypno-conditioner had pumped into him back at Sector X113 before he got fired off into space again. Whatever it was, it had as usual made no impression at all.

The hypnoconditioner was supposed to alter the time-sense, to relax the intellect into a placid exploration of the more charming byways of spatial mathematics or of any other fashionable problem that currently had the planet-bound research teams stumped. As a result, you were expected to end your trip across the stars not only as fresh as if it had begun that same morning but also in an inspired state approaching the level of genius. Giant mental leaps for mankind had been predicted from this treatment, but Randy had yet to hear of a single plus-light traveller emerging from the experience with anything but ideas of the most fundamental nature, inventive as some of these were reputed to have been.

He supposed that somebody somewhere must at last have noticed that plus-light travel seemed to act more as a physical than a mental stimulus, because the more recent Spacegoer's Companions had begun to develop remarkably sophisticated accessories. Computers had always been essential furniture in space, of course, but the new CMP DIRAC–deriv. Mk IV Astg. multi-media computers could provide every imaginable form of entertainment and several unimaginable ones when the pilot ran out of steam. You didn't need to ginger them up with a surreptitious screwdriver like the old models. They were a lot of fun.

Yet even they had their limitations, and after nine months in plus-light with his current Companion, its voluptuous frame enfolding the tiny cabin like an insanely plastic eiderdown, Randy found himself sighing for a reality the computer could never provide. Headed for a particularly obscure K-class star located at the end of the galaxy's spiral arm, he still had to face another nine months of confinement. Books, films, tapes and artworks had been exhausted of their potency, and Randy was reduced to watching the Companion's animated reversioning of Beardsley's 'Under the Hill' illustrations, one of the *Classical Favourites* videotapes. It was evident from the increasingly bizarre departures from the original that the computer shared the pilot's suspicion that his passions might never rise again.

It was at this critical point, so perfectly timed as almost to invite certain conclusions about the computer's motives, that the Companion announced the desirability of a plant call in order to replenish the ship's chemical supplies. A star was located only a few hours distant, possessing an E-type planet stocked with the appropriate materials from which the ship could synthesise what it needed. According to the file, the planet was inhabited by a human-type race at a fairly primitive stage of development; well aware of the strict Federation directives on matters of inter-cultural contact, Randy aimed to land on one of the many uninhabited islands scattered across the oceanic Northern hemisphere.

Finally the computer selected a lush, cone-shaped island which according to the infra-detectors supported no animal life likely to present any major problems, and the ship settled itself down with something of a flourish. The Companions always enjoyed the chance to show off, and landings had been known at which the computers burst out with flags, fireworks, and the Home Planets Anthem, ruining all hopes of peaceful contact with the local life forms. But on this occasion the ship's door merely whispered open and with enormous relief Randy stepped outside.

He was on an open grassy plain close to the sparkling

sapphire sea, a beach of fine white sand crusting its edges. Here and there the grassland featured intriguing pod-shaped plants with superbly velvet green leaves. Occasional trees bore fruits which the Companion stated to be acceptable to the human constitution, and Randy gave them enthusiastic attention; they collapsed succulently in his hands, revealing juices and flesh that were intoxicatingly flavoured. When at last he could eat no more, he ran into the clear, astonishing shallows of the ocean and washed nine months of plus-light from his mind. He rolled in the sun, laughed and shouted, jumped over his own shadow, and did most of the foolish things you'd expect, and in due time he was quiet again, stuck with the one problem that the scents and breezes of the island did nothing to solve.

Part of the trouble was that the ship didn't need him. Its glistening ground serpent, directed by the computer, probed the planet's surface for suitable mineral veins, while the Companion's laboratory section hummed with self-satisfied activity. Samples were tested, ores smelted, reagents mixed and centrifuges whirled; bursts of bluegrass music punctuated the murmuring litany of equations, a racket to which the pilot had become resigned as indication that the computer was deep in thought. He shrugged away the sense of impotence that threatened all too soon to return, and set out to explore the island. It would be good to walk himself into a natural sleep for a change, instead of having to accept one of the computer's nauseating dozee drugs which, whatever the shape and colour (and the range seemed infinite) always gave him nightmares of quite shattering decadence.

The coastline was a delight, composed of clear simple colours in sudden sweeps and curves. A sun of muted gold hung in the sky as though the afternoon would last forever, and the air tasted of perfume, a kind that seemed to bring back unexpected memories of fulfilment. Dreamily following his nose, Randy strolled through a clump of trees that took him out of sight of the ship, and halted abruptly in their shadow while all considerations of the penalties for cultural interference drained from his mind. On the green plain beyond, reality shimmered as if the light-waves themselves were melting in the heat. Then his vision cleared, and there appeared before him, seated on a couch of velvet leaves, a creature of such spectacular beauty that he found himself vowing feverishly never again to waste his time with the 3-D pull-out pin-downs from *Stagman* magazine.

She appeared not to have seen him as she gazed out to sea with mysterious hooded eyes, her body languid and relaxed on the couch. She wore nothing but a short blue shift of some intricately worked material, and the sunlight lapped across her skin to make a tapestry of glowing curves and enticing shadows. Softly Randy moved to her side and amazingly she turned to welcome him, making a tentative movement with her hand which he took as an invitation. He sat down, paused for a moment on the edge of conversation, then reached instead to stroke the dark brown hair that swept like a long veil down her back. Words were unnecessary for the messages pouring between them in the electric air, and the lady showed no sign of wanting a language lesson.

She sighed like the murmur of leaves in midsummer and stretched herself out before him, the hem of her garment rising gently to reveal dark and appetising areas of accessibility. Her scent was all cinnamon, musk, and pure violets, stifling rational thought. Randy toppled drunkenly into her and was enfolded by flesh that writhed delicately against his own, and by hair that seemed to caress him with gently powdered tendrils as he plunged and gasped and shook. The afternoon exploded in golden fragments.

Afterwards, Randy slid from the couch and lay on the white sand convinced, as the Companion had never been able to convince him, that he now stood a chance of understanding his place in the universe. It was as though beings from some outer galaxy were suddenly aware of his presence, but as they stirred to greet him he began to fear the hollow echo of their thoughts, the dissonant music of their knowledge, and he sank back into wakefulness. A mist of writhing green and purple shapes lay briefly over his eyes, and warning voices whispered instantly forgotten messages. But the girl still sat placidly on her couch and at the sight of her, Randy's confusion melted away. Purpose and anticipation pulled him briskly to his feet.

To his surprise, her welcome was not repeated. She smiled in an absent-minded fashion and returned her gaze to the ocean. When he tried to caress her as before, her flesh seemed actually to crawl with distaste, she made no move to lie back, and her shift stayed clamped demurely to her knees. Randy was half inclined to force the issue, but the Federation directives had once more begun to hover at the back of his mind and at last he gave up. Promising to return soon with priceless gifts, an offer to which she paid not the slightest attention, he resumed his exploration of the island.

The coastline dipped again, and the girl soon disappeared behind him. The rich grass rippled in the heat and the air quivered with a spice that made his blood surge; beside him, the ocean flashed a million reflections of the sky. Shading his eyes, he blinked with disbelief at a new girl who lay ahead on her couch of velvet, her body undulating in unmistakable delight at his approach. She could have been the sister of the gorgeous creature he had just left; the same dark hair cascaded over the same perfect slopes of the back, the same kaleidoscope of delicate lights and shadows was picked out by the sun across the smooth and supple limbs, the same sweet savour drifted teasingly across the grass. She even wore a similar shift, although this one was red. It was intricately textured with tiny patterns that changed and flowed as he tried to follow them, their writhing designs suggesting an elusive and haunting symbolism.

Disinclined to question the gifts that fate so seldom placed in his path, Randy made reverent haste towards the startlingly beautiful phenomenon that awaited him. Again words could be discarded as unnecessary; her eyes, deep violet pools of promise, beckoned him with unequivocal invitations, fully reinforced by the receptive and compliant body. He became mindless, drawn into a frenzy of sensations that mingled and mounted, until a nova flared and he sank at last into a dreamlike state where the girl's every movement and gesture seemed part of an obscure but vital communication between one end of the universe and the other. He stared fascinated into her eyes, while a haze of glorious colours spiralled around the couch, and then he must have slept, for there was a time when the grasses and creepers that carpeted the island appeared to explore him with their tendrils and the moss grew restless beneath his back. The sun was a deeper gold and had dipped lower in the sky when Randy splashed ocean over his head and returned refreshed to his delightful partner.

Close to her, he found desire reviving as strongly as if it had never been satisfied, but when he reached again for the girl she was as unyielding as a block of wood, and her gaze was coldly out to sea. Try as he might, he was unable to rekindle her interest in the healthy athletic pursuits he had in mind. She ignored him so completely that he couldn't even be sure she understood what he wanted. Eventually Randy decided he would have to leave her there and hope she'd be around next day in more amenable mood. He kissed the motionless mouth and wandered back in the direction of the ship.

He splashed in the shallows along the dappled coast, the sand crunching beneath his feet, the breeze stirring across the grass dunes and probing the clumps of trees. The girl in the blue shift was still sunbathing where he had left her, and he halted on the edge of the water, uncertain whether to wave and rush by or stop to talk about old times.

Her perfume settled the matter. As he approached, led by the nose, she stirred and stretched and her smile got inside his body and tuned it up like an orchestra. She reached for him with irresistible urgency and once more he felt himself swept into her on an unthinking torrent of enjoyment. Ripping away the shift completely, he abandoned himself to an extraordinary symphony of exotic rhythms and caresses. It was as if the planet itself had opened up to swallow him, the grass and the giant green leaves closing above his head.

The climax seemed to scatter him around the landscape like fragments of a bursting pod. For a long time he lay unable to move, with fantastic visions of strange beings and unearthly music wandering through his mind. The colours of the waning afternoon ran slowly together into a magnificent sunset, and when he finally staggered to his feet it was growing dark. The girl lay on her couch in a tight ball and he could do nothing to rouse her. Reluctant to carry her back to the ship and risk arousing the Companion's suspicion about his illegal activities, he draped the torn shift and some of the big velvet leaves over her as some form of protection against the night, and made his way alone across the grass.

The computer was rather stuffy about having been left on its own for so long but at last it consented, after some argument, to turn the lights out. Randy fell instantly asleep on his bunk as dozee capsules bounced unheeded across his chest to the floor.

When he awoke the next morning, the Companion was strangely silent, although lights pulsed here and there on its console. The datadials indicated that the task of chemical re-stocking was now complete, but there was no indication that any resumption of the journey had been calculated. Debating whether to give the thing a kick in the fusebox, Randy suddenly noticed that the ship's door was wide open, revealing sea and sand and sunlight. The spiced air of the island summoned him, and gladly he responded.

It was crowded out there. Green couches were spread around in the sun, thickly clustered near the ship but also dotted across the grass in all directions as far as Randy could see, covering the island. And on them reclined girls of every description, of all sizes, all colours. They all wore shifts of the familiar design, in hues of rainbow miscellany, although red and blue were obvious favourites. Otherwise the girls were only alike in that they were blindingly beautiful and their deep clear eyes were fixed on Randy as if their lives had been specially constructed for this one ecstatic moment. As he appeared, a wave of delight surged across his audience, and he thought he heard the island itself sigh in the shimmering silence of the morning. His fans were waiting and there was much to be done. Their perfume tugged him forward.

For several hours, Randy was extremely busy. Arms, bodies and legs ensnared him in a thicket of willing flesh, and hunger and pleasure pursued each other with frantic urgency. He ploughed and dug his way across this incredible plantation of sunsoaked skin, discarded garments, and voluptuous welcome, until his responses became too painful to be worth the continuing effort, and the pauses between bouts were shadowed with uneasy dreams in which his whole being became fragmented and seemed to crumble into sand with untraceable finality. Dimly he congratulated himself on his performance, and at last he ventured to hope that he might spend the rest of his days without again setting eyes on another female form.

Breaking free from the eager ranks of his admirers, he splashed and floated in the warm ocean until a modest confidence returned to his legs that they could hold him upright once more. The girls fortunately made no attempt to follow him, but gazed in worship from the shoreline, undulating pensively on their couches. Randy chewed some fruit and wandered at the water's edge, keeping out of reach; maintaining a polite smile, he eyed the girls dispassionately and did some hard thinking.

Suddenly he noticed among the sunbathers the girl in blue he had left wrapped in leaves the night before. Evidently her night out had proved far from beneficial. She lay apart from the others, unmoving on the stained and fraying couch, her shift draped over her limbs like a rotten shroud. The tawny skin that had shone out to him yesterday was now pallid and dull, sagging in places to create hollows of emaciation, and her mane of dark hair had coagulated into a limp, repellent mess. Horrified at this apparent consequence of his attentions, Randy made his way towards her; the Companion had assured him that under normal circumstances there could be no possible compatibility between the local bacteria and Randy's own collection of extra-galactic viruses, but the circumstances had strayed rather far from the normal. If the girl was in trouble, Randy was likely to be in trouble too.

In the first automatic move of diagnosis, he took her hand. It parted immediately from the sagging mass of her body and rested soggily in his grip, greenish matter dripping from the severed wrist. The fingers broke and oozed together in his palm, and the thumb dropped to the ground with a soft squelch. Shaking off the decaying tissue in revulsion, he turned the girl's face towards him. It slipped under his touch, and his fingers sank into the black jelly where her eyes had been.

Randy left in a hurry, clambering heedlessly across a landscape of enchanting smiles. The island heaved beneath his feet, and the sun beat like a hammer on his skull. When he got to the ship he was crawling and had the impression that he was making a lot of noise. He fell through the doorway and dragged the hatch shut.

The computer received Randy's confession in utter contempt. If he had only bothered, said the Companion, to study all the information available before charging out of the ship like some Jugoslavian nudist (the doubtless apocryphal ardour of this legendary race was the basis for one of the more memorable sagas of the spaceways), he might have avoided making so spectacular a fool of himself. He should be aware, added the Companion, that nothing was unknown to or unforeseen by the CMP DIRAC–deriv. Mk IV Astg. multi-media computers, and that exploits such as Randy's not only had no hope of being kept secret but were even so predictable as to be exactly calculable according to a now-proven constant in which x was equal to fifteen plus-light square roots divided simultaneously by point seven recurring. During the hours in which Randy had been neglecting his duties, stated the Companion, it had taken the opportunity to prepare a thesis on this very subject, demonstrating a breadth of vision so extraordinary that the Companion made so bold as to be confident that the highest intergalactic honours would be accorded to it when the voyage was completed. With a modest cough, the Companion disgorged a six-hundred-page volume of computer print-outs, handsomely bound in leather with gold edgings. Randy might care, suggested the Companion, to browse through this epoch-making work while preparing his own report to the Federation, although they were unlikely to treat his case with much sympathy if he presented it in his usual inarticulate manner.

Wearily dropping the book into the recycler, Randy pressed the Bowman button (the emergency control known only to the pilot in plus-light ships), and let the Companion sing nursery rhymes for half an hour while he consumed a soothe-tube of nerve paste. Relaxing on the control couch, he then re-engaged the information banks of the computer and summoned up all available facts and references about the planet they were on. The Companion had neglected to mention, of course, that the place had actually been visited before, so that instead of the usual brief list of aerial survey data there were voluminous technical and ecological reports, mostly incomprehensible to the non-specialist. They rolled across the information screen and Randy scowled his way through them without finding anything helpful. Such biological deductions as had been made seemed in no way related to his own experiences, and only one group of the exploring team had been anywhere near the islands of the Northern hemisphere, their purpose and conclusions connected merely with the botanical.

After presenting all the main texts, the computer automatically began to turn up the footnotes and addenda. Letting these run at double speed, Randy was about to give up hope when a small picture flashed by that struck a faint chord. He turned back and stared for a long time. The brightly coloured illustration showed the cross-section of a flower, and the accompanying article, under a severe Latin headline, was a report by one of the botanists.

Of the three species of *Bacchantius* growing on the planet Rosy Lee, perhaps the most unusual is *Gigantiflora*. The plant is herbaceous, and perenniates by means of thick starchy tubers. It flowers annually in the correct conditions and is a member of the family *Phorusorchidacae*, the local orchid family. (See ref. Axaia p. 74,418 for description of the parallel evolution of flowering plants on E-type worlds. See ref. Modoinisk p. 731,111 for detailed parameters of E-type conditions.)

Normally the *Gigantiflora* flowers only after sensing the airborne waste products of the humanoid species *Gaggus gaggus* which inhabits the planet Rosy Lee. The buds take some five months to mature but require no external stimulus to begin formation. When fully developed, they lie dormant under a thick covering of velvety green leaves. Once the presence of a humanoid has aroused the flowering response the buds rise above the leaves overnight and open just before dawn. The flowers are huge and strikingly shaped. Specimens examined ranged from 1·3716 m to 1·8315 m in height.

Pollination is by pseudo-copulation, as in many species of plant, but is exceptional in this case in that the pollinating agent is the male *Gaggus*. The flowers are exact replicas of native women, and their whole structure, composed of united sepals and petals, is complete in almost every external detail. One of the few visible differences is the threadlike though robust stem emerging from the small of the plant's back.

The petal, analogous to the lip in other *orchidacae*, is primarily bright red or blue, although other shades based on these colours can often be found. Giving the appearance of a short garment, it is united to the perianth only by a tiny join at the nape of the neck and may be removed completely without any noticeable damage, although it quickly shrivels.

The flowers have a very powerful scent, and while the chemical structure of this has yet to be determined it is known to have pronounced hallucinatory and aphrodisiacal properties, which it is thought acted originally to prevent the *Gaggus* from discovering the true nature of the girl that apparently confronts him. Under the influence of the scent, for example, the male finds the eyes of the plant lifelike and mobile, whereas in reality they are the least successful part of the imitation.

Capable of a quite sophisticated series of mechanical movements and reactions, *Gigantiflora* will on being disturbed by a suitable stimulus go through motions resembling those of a primitive coquette. The native male *Gaggus* is often completely addicted to the pleasures afforded by these flowers, to the extent that he will neglect his own wife. The female *Gaggus*, on the other hand, destroys these plants whenever she finds them. The theory appears tenable that the population of Rosy Lee is maintained at a low level by the waste of male effort expended on cultivating *Gigantiflora*.

The pollen develops before the gynoceum and forms a thick powder on the plant's 'pubic' area. During pseudo-copulation this pollen adheres to the male, and when next he amuses himself with a *Gigantiflora* it is transferred to the area surrounding the new flower's 'navel' – which is in fact the stigma, thus completing the pollination. Directly after this process the flower is able to discourage further attempts by the same male, becoming rigid and unapproachable so that self-pollination is avoided.

The seeds of the plant are dust-like and blow many miles, even across oceans. On some of the planet's many uninhabited islands, whole colonies of the plants may be found; as the *Gaggus* is disinclined to travel, lacking any great incentive or energy to do so, these colonies presumably never reach the flowering stage. When members of the present expedition landed on one such island, the flowers appeared by the second day in numbers approaching infestation proportions, the effect resembling that of an overcrowded brothel. Since the team was wholly female, it was not possible to judge the effect on a male, but the sight, smell, and hallucinatory vapours were such as to convince us that the effect would be overpowering even for a civilized man.

I must confess (the report added, taking a suddenly personal tone), that while as a botanist I found the flowers fascinating, as a woman I found them profoundly disturbing, almost disgusting. Even when I was cutting portions of the petal from the 'face', an unsettling exercise, the plant's lower half made several attempts to seduce me, although as far as we were aware only males could inspire the pollination mechanism. The fact that in uninhabited regions the flowers might react to women as well leads to interesting speculation about alternative means of pollination. And although every member of our team professed disgust for the flowers, several plants unquestionably set seed during our stay on the island despite the impossibility of self-pollination.

Further research could doubtless be pursued in this area, but while this would be diverting enough for the specialists involved, no particular value can be anticipated from it. We are familiar in botany with the basic principles of pseudo-copulation, studied in detail on Terra in the last century. (Ref: *Wild Flowers of the World* by Everard & Morley, reprinted under the *Treasures of Antiquity* label: 'The insect-like form of the lip and the scent of the flower in the *Ophrys* attract the males of certain insects and stimulates them into abortive attempts at copulation. During this pseudo-copulation the insects pick up pollinia or transfer pollen to the stigmas. Some tropical orchids have likewise been shown to possess particular scents which excite insects sexually.') A Research Priority Rating is accordingly recommended at no more than Z-Grade.

Some technicalities followed about the morphology and cytology of the plant, but Randy had read far enough. His head hurt as a torrent of ideas and schemes poured through his mind, and he realized that the hypnoconditioning he'd gone through at Sector X113 was, thanks to his uniquely exhausted condition, at last getting the chance to work. In dizzy flashes of inspiration, he saw that he was destined to become the greatest gardener ever known. He grabbed a screwdriver and got started.

The rest of course is history. Randy waited on Rosy Lee long enough to collect the ten pods of seeds he was later to refer to in his autobiography as his offspring, and within a few months he appeared on the 'dry' planet Bergia (where prostitution is illegal) as the proprietor of 'The Pleasure Gardens of Rosy Lee'. The uproar led to a court case, a magnificent specimen of *Bacchantius Gigantiflora* was produced before the enraptured judge, and all charges were dismissed. The galaxy rang with the news, and Randy's fortune was made.

He was able to make the unprecedented purchase of a plus-light ship – his own – from the Federation, complete with Ship's Companion.

Plus-light travel being as complicated as it is, few were in a position to track down the planet where Randy got his supplies, but those who made it to the islands of Rosy Lee said they found there only desert scrubland and bleak crags. The place had an atmosphere of terror, they said, and they were glad to leave; the *Gaggus* population, however, seemed undisturbed despite the odd preference on the part of the males for a species of cauliflower with a stench like rotten pulp.

It seems that Randy and his screwdriver, whirled to the heights of creativity by the hypnoconditioning that ran through his brain, had converted the Ship's Companion to new levels of chemical accomplishment. When the computer had finished with Rosy Lee, the aphrodisiac breeze that drifted across the planet had acquired a tang that went unnoticed by the *Gaggus* nose but which filled the human senses with stark revulsion. Thus Randy and his brood could preserve a comfortable monopoly. The Companion, too, proved to be an unrivalled teacher; the girls in the 'Pleasure Gardens', now a universal attraction, are renowned as much for their seductive conversation as for their physical skills. Naturally they are all experts in bluegrass music. And the hybrid strains developed with the aid of the computer become more delectable year by year, especially those highly prized specimens reputed to resemble famous beauties of the past. The Cleopatra Convulser, the Bardot Brainstorm, and the Lovelace Paralyzer have passed into legend.

So that, girls, is the story of the famed horticulturalist Randy Richmond, known throughout the galaxy (although the plus-light pilots have, I believe, a slightly different version) as 'Mr Greenfingers'. All strength to his compost, and may his flyspray never dwindle! Now, dig in. Another batch of conservationists just stopped by our greenhouse.

By the Seashore
R. A. Lafferty

The most important event in the life of Oliver Murex was his finding of a seashell when he was four years old. It was a bright and shining shell that the dull little boy found. It was bigger than his own head (and little Oliver had an unusually large head), and had two eyes peering out of its mantle cavity that were brighter and more intelligent-seeming than Oliver's own. Both Oliver and the shell had these deep, black, shiny eyes that were either mockingly lively or completely dead – with such shiny, black things it was hard to say which.

That big shell was surely the brightest thing on that sunny morning beach and no one could have missed it. But George, Hector, August, Mary, Catherine and Helen had all of them missed it and they were older and sharper-eyed than was Oliver. They had been looking for bright shells, going in a close skirmish line over that sand and little Oliver had been trailing them with absent mind and absent eyes.

'Why do you pick up all the dumb little ones and leave the good big one?' he yiped from their rear. They turned and saw the shell and they were stunned. It actually was stunning in appearance – why hadn't they seen it? (It had first to be seen by one in total sympathy with it. Then it could be seen by any superior person.)

'I wouldn't have seen it either if it hadn't whistled at me,' Oliver said.

'It's a Hebrew Volute,' George cried out, 'and they're not even found in this part of the world.'

'It isn't. It's a Music Volute,' Mary contradicted.

'I think that it's a Neptune Volute,' Hector hazarded.

'I wish I could say that it's a Helen Volute,' Helen said, 'but it isn't. It's not a Volute at all. It's a Cone, an Alphabet Cone.'

Now these were the shelliest kids along the seashore that summer and they should all have known a Volute from a Cone, all except little Oliver. How could there be such wide differences among them?

'Helen is right about its being a Cone,' August said. 'But it isn't an Alphabet Cone. It's a Barthelemy Cone, a big one.'

'It's a Prince Cone,' Catherine said simply. But they were all wrong. It was a deadly Geography Cone, even though it was three times too big to be one. How could such sharp-eyed children not recognize such an almost legendary prize?

Oliver kept this cone shell with him all the years of his growing up. He listened often to the distant sounding in it, as people have always listened to seashells. No cone, however, is a real ocean-roarer of a shell. They haven't the far crash; they haven't the boom. They just are not shaped for it, not like a Conch, not like a Vase Shell, not like a Scallop, not even like the common Cowries or Clam Shells or Helmet Shells. Cones make rather intermittent, sharp sounds, not really distant. They tick rather than roar.

'Other shells roar their messages from way off,' Helen said once. 'Cones telegraph theirs.' And the clicking, ticking of Cones does sound somewhat like the chatter of a telegraph.

Some small boys have toy pandas or bears. But Oliver Murex had this big seashell for his friend and toy and security. He slept with it – he carried it with him always. He depended on it. If he was asked a question he would first hold the big cone shell to his ear and listen – then he would answer the question intelligently. But if for any reason he did not have his shell near at hand he seemed incapable of an intelligent answer on any subject.

There would sometimes be a splatter of small blotches or dusty motes on the floor or table near the shell.

'Oh, let me clean those whatever-they-ares away,' mother

Murex said once when she was nozzling around with the cleaner.

'No, no – leave them alone – they'll go back in,' Oliver protested. 'They just came out to get a little sunlight.' And the little blotches, dust motes, fuzz, stains, whatever retreated into the shell of the big cone.

'Why, they're alive!' the mother exclaimed.

'Isn't everybody?' Oliver asked.

'It is an Alphabet Cone just as I always said it was,' Helen declared. 'And those little skittering things are the letters of the different alphabets that fall off the outside of the shell. The cone has to swallow them again each time, and when it has digested them they will come through to the outside again where they can be seen in their patterns.'

Helen still believed this was an Alphabet Cone. It wasn't. It was a deadly Geography Cone. The little blotches that seemed to fall off it or to come out of it and run around – and that then had to be swallowed again – may have been little continents or seas coming from the Geography Cone; they may have been quite a number of different things. But if they were alphabets (well, they *were* those, among other things), then they were more highly complex alphabets than Helen suspected.

It isn't necessary that all children in a family be smart. Six smart ones out of seven isn't bad. The family could afford big-headed, queer-eyed Oliver, even if he seemed a bit retarded. He could get by most of the time. If he had his shell with him, he could get by all the time.

One year in grade school, though, they forbade him the company of his shell. And he failed every course abysmally.

'I see Oliver's problem as a lack of intelligence,' his teacher told father Murex. 'And lack of intelligence is usually found in the mind.'

'I didn't expect it to be found in his feet,' Oliver's father said. But he did get a psychologist in to go over his slow son from head to foot.

'He's a bit different from a schizo,' the psychologist said

when he had finished the examination. 'What he has is two concentric personalities. We call them the core personality and the mantle personality – and there is a separation between them. The mantle or outer personality is dull in Oliver's case. The core personality is bright enough, but it is able to contact the outer world only by means of some separate object. I believe that the unconscious of Oliver is now located in this object and his intelligence is tied to it. That seashell there, now, is quite well balanced mentally. It's too bad that it isn't a boy. Do you have any idea what object it is that Oliver is so attached to?'

'It's that seashell there. He's had it quite a while. Should I get rid of it?'

'That's up to you. Many fathers would say yes in such case; almost as many would say no. If you get rid of the shell the boy will die. But then the problem will be solved – you'll no longer have a problem child.'

Mr Murex sighed, and he thought about it. He had decisions to make all day long and he disliked having to make them in the evening, too.

'I guess the answer is no,' he finally said. 'I'll keep the seashell and I'll also keep the boy. They're both good conversation pieces. Nobody else has anything that looks like either of them.'

Really they had come to look alike. Oliver and his shell, both big-headed and bug-eyed and both of them had a quiet and listening air about them.

Oliver did quite well in school after they let him have the big seashell with him in class again.

A man was visiting in the Murex house one evening. This man was by hobby a conchologist or student of seashells. He talked about shells. He set out some little shells that he had carried wrapped in his pocket and explained them. Then he noticed Oliver's big seashell and he almost ruptured a posterior adductor muscle.

'It's a Geography Cone!' he shrieked. 'A giant one! And it's alive!'

'I think it's an Alphabet Cone,' Helen said.

'I think it's a Prince Cone,' Catherine said.

'No, no, it's a Geography Cone and it's alive!'

'Oh, I've suspected for a long time that it was alive,' Papa Murex said.

'But don't you understand? It's a giant specimen of the deadly Geography Cone.'

'Yes, I think so. Nobody else has one,' father Murex said.

'What do you keep in it?' the conchologist chattered. 'What do you feed it?'

'Oh, it has total freedom here, but it doesn't move around very much. We don't feed it anything at all. It belongs to my son Oliver. He puts it to his ear and listens to it often.'

'Great galloping gastropods, man! It's likely to take an ear clear off the boy.'

'It never has.'

'But it's deadly poisonous. People have died of its sting.'

'I don't believe any one of our family ever has. I'll ask my wife. Oh, no, I needn't. I'm sure none of my family has ever died of its sting. I just remembered that none of them has ever died at all.'

The man with the hobby of conchology didn't visit the Murex house very much after that. He was afraid of that big seashell.

One day the school dentist gave a curious report of things going on in Oliver's mouth.

'Little crabs are eating the boy's teeth – little microscopic crabs,' the dentist (he was a nervous man) told Mr Murex.

'I never heard of microscopic crabs,' Mr Murex said. 'Have you seen them, really, or examined them at all?'

'Oh, no, I haven't seen them. How would I see them? But his teeth just look as if microscopic crabs had been eating them. Ah, I'm due for a vacation. I was going to leave next week.'

'Are the teeth deteriorating fast?' Mr Murex asked the dentist.

'No, that's what puzzles me,' the dentist said. 'They're not deteriorating. The enamel is disappearing, eaten by small crabs, I'm sure of that; but it's being replaced by something else, by some shell-like material.'

'Oh, it's all right then,' Mr Murex said.

'I was going to leave on vacation next week. I'll call someone and tell them that I'm leaving right now,' the dentist said.

The dentist left, and he never did return to his job or to his home. It was later heard of him that he had first abandoned dentistry and then life.

But little Oliver grew up, or anyhow he grew out. He seemed to be mostly head, and his dwarfish body was not much more than an appendage. He and the great seashell came to look more and more like each other by the day.

'I swear, sometimes I can't tell which of you is Oliver,' Helen Murex said one day. She was more fond of Oliver and his shell than were any of their brothers or sisters. 'Which of you is?' she asked.

'I am.'

Oliver Geography Cone grinned.

'I am.'

Oliver Murex grinned.

Oliver Murex was finally out of school and had taken his place in the family business. The Murex family was big in communications, the biggest in the world, really. Oliver had an office just off the office of his father. Not much was expected of him. He seemed still to be a dull boy, but very often he gave almost instant answers to questions that no one else could answer in less than a week or more. Well, it was either Oliver or his shell who gave the almost instant answers. They had come to resemble each other in voice almost as much as in appearance and the father really didn't care which of them answered – as long as the answers were quick and correct. And they were both.

'Oliver has a girl friend,' Helen teased one day. 'She says she's going to marry him.'

'However would he get a girl friend?' brother Hector asked, puzzled.

'Yes. How is it possible?' Mr. Murex wanted to know.

'After all, we *are* very rich,' Helen reminded them.

'Oh, I didn't know that the younger generation had any interest in money,' Mr Murex said.

'And, after all, she *is* Brenda Frances,' Helen said.

'Oh, yes – I've noticed that she does have an interest in money,' Mr Murex said. 'Odd that such a recessive trait should crop up in a young lady of today.'

Brenda Frances worked for the Murex firm.

Brenda Frances wanted round-headed Oliver for the money that might attach to him, but she didn't want a lot of gaff that seemed also to attach to the young fellow. But now Oliver became really awake for the first time in his life, stimulated by Brenda Frances' apparent interest. He even waxed a little bit arty and poetic when he talked to her, mostly about his big seashell.

'Do you know that he wasn't native to the sea or shore where we found him,' Oliver said. 'He tells me that he comes from the very far north, from the Sea of Moyle.'

'Damn that bug-eyed seashell!' Brenda Frances complained. 'He almost looks alive. I don't mind being leered at by men, but I dislike being leered at by a seashell. I don't believe that there is any such thing as the Sea of Moyle. I never heard of it. There isn't any sea in the very far north except the Arctic Ocean.'

'Oh, but he says that this is very very far north,' Oliver said with his ear to the shell (*When you two put your heads together like that I don't know whose ear is listening to whose shell*, Helen had said once), 'very, very far north – and perhaps very again. It's far, far beyond the Arctic Ocean.'

'You can't get any farther north than the Arctic,' Brenda Frances insisted. 'It's as far north as there is any north.'

'No. He says that the Sea of Moyle is much farther,' Oliver repeated the whispers and tickings of the shell. 'I think probably the Sea of Moyle is clear off-world.'

'Oh great glabrous glabula!' Brenda Frances swore. Things weren't going well here. There was so much nonsense about Oliver as nearly to nullify the pleasant prospect of money.

'Did you know that he has attendants?' Oliver asked. 'Very small attendants.'

'Like fleas?'

'Like crabs. They really are crabs, almost invisible, almost microscopic fiddler crabs. They are named Gelasimus Notarii or Annotating Crabs – I don't know why. They live in his mouth and stomach most of the time, but they come out when they're off duty. They do a lot of work for him. They do all his paper work and they are very handy. I've been practising with them for a long time, too, but I haven't learned to employ them at all well yet.'

'Oh great whelping whelks!' Brenda Frances sputtered.

'Did you know that the old Greeks shipped wine in cone shells?' Oliver asked. 'They did it because cone shells are so much bigger on the inside than on the outside. They would put half a dozen cone shells into an amphora of wine to temper them for it. Then they would take them out and pour one, two, or three amphoras of wine into each cone shell. The cones have so many internal passages that there is no limit to their capacity. The Greeks would load ships with the wine-filled cones and ship them all over the world. By using cones, they could ship three times as much wine as otherwise in the same ship.'

'Wino seashells, that's what we really need,' Brenda Frances mumbled insincerely.

'I'll ask him,' Oliver said. They put their two heads together, Oliver and the cone shell. 'He says that cones hardly ever become winos,' Oliver announced then. 'He says that they can take it or leave it alone.'

'After we are married you will have to stop this silly talk,' Brenda Frances said. 'Where do you get it anyhow?'

'From Shell. I'll tell you something else. The Greek friezes and low reliefs that some students of shells study – they are natural and not carved. And they aren't really Greek things. They're pictures of some off-world things that look kind of Greek. They're not even pictures of people. They're pictures of some kind of seaweed from the Sea of Moyle that looks like Earth people. I hope that clears up that mystery.'

'Oliver, I have plans for us,' Brenda Frances said firmly, 'and the plans seem very hard to put across to you in words. I have always believed that a half-hour's intimacy is worth more than forever's talk. Come along now. We're alone except for old sea-slob there.'

'I'd better ask my mother first,' Oliver said. 'It seems that there is some question about this intimacy bit, a question that they all believed would never arise in my case. I'd better ask her.'

'Your mother is visiting her sister at Peach Beach,' Brenda Frances said. 'Your father is fishing at Cat Island. George and Hector and August are all off on sales trips. Mary and Catherine and Helen are all making political appearances somewhere. This is the first time they've all been out of town at once. I came to you so you wouldn't be lonesome.'

'I'm never lonesome with Shell. You think the intimacy thing will be all right, then?'

'I sure do doubt it, but it's worth a try,' Brenda Frances said. 'For me, you're the likeliest jackpot in town. Where else would I find such a soft head with so much money attached?'

'We read a seduction scene in a book once,' Oliver said. 'It was kind of funny and kind of fun.'

'Who's *we*?'

'Shell and myself.'

'After we're married, we're sure going to change that "we" stuff,' Brenda Frances said. 'But how does Shell read?'

'With his eyes like everyone else. And the annotating crabs

correlate the reading for him. He says that seduction scenes are more fun where he comes from. All the seductors gather at the first high tide after the big moon is full. The fellows are on one side of the tidal basin – and then their leader whistles and they put their milt in the tidewater. And the she seashells (Earth usage – they don't call themselves that there), who are on the other side of the tidal basin, put their roe into the water. Then the she seashell leader whistles an answer and that is the seduction. It's better when both moons are still in the sky. At the Sea of Moyle they have two moons.'

'Come along, Oliver,' Brenda Frances said, 'and you can whistle if you want to, but that seawash talk has got to stop.' She took big-headed, short-legged Oliver under her arm and went with him to the chamber she had selected as the seduction room. And Shell followed along.

'How does it walk without any legs?' Brenda Frances asked.

'He doesn't walk. He just moves. I'm getting so I can move that way too.'

'It's not going to get into bed with us, Oliver?'

'Yes, but he says he'll just watch the first time. You don't send him at all.'

'Oh, all right. But I tell you, there's going to be some changes around here after we're married.'

She turned out the lights when she was ready. But they hadn't been in the dark for five seconds when Brenda Frances began to complain.

'Why is the bed so slimy all at once?'

'Shell likes it that way. It reminds him more of the ocean.'

'Ouch! Great crawling crawdads – something is biting me! Are they bugs?'

'No, no – they're the little crabs,' Oliver told her. 'But Shell says that they only bite people they don't like.'

'Wow, let me sweep them out of this bed.'

'You can't. They're almost too little to see and they hang on. Besides, they have to be here.'

'Why?'

'They're annotating crabs. They take notes.'

Brenda Frances left the bed and the house in a baffled fury. 'Best jackpot in town, hell!' she said. 'There are other towns. Somewhere there's another half-brained patsy in a monied family – one that won't bring the whole damned ocean to bed with him.'

It was later learned that Brenda Frances left town in the same fury.

'That was an even less satisfying seduction scene than in that book,' Shell and his crabby minions conveyed. 'We do these things so much better on the Sea of Moyle.'

So Oliver preserved his virtue. After all, he was meant for other things.

An off-world person of another great and rich family in the communications field came to call on Mr Murex at his home.

'We weren't expecting your arrival in quite such manner,' Mr Murex said. He had no idea of how the other had arrived – he simply was there.

'Oh, I didn't want to wait for a vehicle. They're too slow. I conveyed myself,' the visitor said. They met as tycoon to tycoon. Mr Murex was very anxious that he and his family should make a good impression on their distinguished visitor. He even thought about concealing Oliver, but that would have been a mistake.

'That is a fine specimen,' the visiting person said. 'Fine. He could almost be from back home.'

'He is my son Oliver,' said Mr Murex, quite pleased.

'And his friend there,' the visitor continued, 'I swear that he is from back home.'

'There's a misunderstanding,' Mr Murex said. 'The other one there is a seashell.'

'What is a seashell?' the visitor asked. 'Are Earth seas hatched out of shells? How odd. But you are mistaken, person Murex. That *is* a specimen from back home. Do you have the papers on him?'

'I don't know of any papers. What would such papers indicate?'

'Oh, that you have given fair exchange for the specimen. We wouldn't want an interworld conflict over such a small matter, would we?'

'If you will let me know what this "fair exchange" is – ' Mr Murex tried to comply.

'Oh, I'll let you know at the time of my leaving,' the visiting tycoon said. 'We'll settle on something.' This person was very much up on communications. He engaged Mr Murex and George, Mary, Hector, Catherine, August, Helen, yes and Oliver, all in simultaneous conversations on the subject. And he made simultaneous deals so rapid-fire as to astound all of them. He controlled even more patents than did the Murex family, some of them overlapping. The two tycoons were making non-conflict territory agreements and the visitor was out-shuffling the whole Murex clan by a little bit in these complex arrangements.

'Oh, just let me clean them off there!' Mrs Murex said once where she saw a splatter of small blotches and dust motes on the table that served both for conference and dinner table – the splatter of little things was mostly about the visitor.

'No, no, leave them,' that person said. 'I enjoy their conversation. Really, they could almost be Notarii from my own world.' Things began then to go well in these transactions even for the Murex family, just when they had seemed to be going poorly.

The visitor was handsome in an off-worldly way. He was toothless, but his bony upper and lower beak cut through everything, through the prime steak that seemed too tough to the Murex clan, through the bones, through the plates. 'Glazed, baked clay, we use it too. It spices a meal,' the visitor said of the plates as he munched them. 'And you have designs and colours on the pieces. We do that sometimes with cookies.'

'They are priceless chinaware,' Mrs Murex said in a voice that was almost a complaint.

'Yes, priceless, delicious, exquisite,' the visitor said. 'Now shall we finalize the contracts and agreements?'

Several waiting stenographers came in with their machines. Brenda Frances was not among them – she had left the Murex firm and left town. The stenographers began to take down the contracts and agreements on their dactyl-tactiles.

'And I'll just save time and translation by giving the whole business in my own language to this stenographer from my own world,' the visiting tycoon said.

'Ah, that isn't a stenographer there, however much it may remind you of the stenographers where you come from.' Mr Murex tried to set a matter straight again. 'That is what we call a seashell.'

But the visiting tycoon spoke in his own language to Shell. And Shell whistled. Then whole blotches and clouds of the almost invisible annotating crabs rushed into Shell, ready to work. The visiting tycoon spoke rapidly in off-worldly language, his beak almost touching Shell.

'Ah, the Geography Cone shell – that's what that thing is – is said to be absolutely deadly,' Mr Murex tried to warn the visitor.

'They only kill people they don't like,' the visitor said and he went on with his business.

The annotating crabs did the paper work well. Completed contracts and agreements began to roll out of the mantle cavity of Shell. And all the business was finished in one happy glow.

'That is it,' the visiting tycoon said with complete satisfaction after all the papers were mutually signed. With his beak he bit a very small ritual wedge from the cheek of his hostess, Mrs Murex. That was a parting custom where he came from.

'And now "fair exchange" for the specimen from back home,' he said. 'I always find these exchanges satisfying and fruitful.'

He had a sack. And he put the short-legged, big-headed Oliver into that sack.

'Oh, that's not fair exchange,' Mr Murex protested. 'I know he looks a little unusual, but that is my son Oliver.'

'He's fair enough exchange,' the visitor said. He didn't wait for a vehicle. They were too slow. He conveyed himself. And he and Oliver were gone.

So all that the Murex family had to remind them of their vanished son and brother was that big seashell, the Geography Cone. Was it really from the world of the visitor? Who knows the true geography of the Geography Cone?

Oliver sat on the shore of the Sea of Moyle in the far, far north. This was not in the cold, far north. It was on a warm and sunny beach in the off-world far north. And Oliver sat there as if he belonged.

There hadn't been any sudden space-change in Oliver. There had been only the slow change through all the years of his life and that was never a great alteration – a great difference hadn't been needed in him.

Oliver was bright and shining, the brightest thing on that sunny morning beach. He had his big head and his little body. He had two shiny black eyes peering out of his mantle cavity. Oliver was very much a seashell now, a special and prized shell. (They didn't use that term there, though. Seashell? Was the Sea of Moyle hatched out of a shell?)

Six sharp-eyed children of the dominant local species were going in close skirmish right over that sunny sand and a smaller seventh child trailed them with absent mind and absent eyes. The big moon had already gone down; the little moon still hung low in the sky like a silver coin. And the sun was an overpowering gold.

The sharp-eyed children were looking for bright shore specimens and they were finding them, too. And right ahead of them was that almost legendary prize, a rare Oliver Cone.

Hardcastle
Ron Goulart

The house had a slight German accent.

Bob Lambrick had just landed his helicopter on the copter deck next to the low rambling ranch-style house and he was climbing down out of the ship, his portfolio and attaché case hugged under his left arm.

'I was about to kiss that orange tree goodbye,' said the house from the speaker mounted in the bird feeder in one of the decorative pines beyond the landing area.

Bob glanced at the orange tree on his front quarter acre. A long orange was rolling across the bright grass and toward the edge of the hillside. It tumbled on over and fell two hundred feet down to the Pacific Ocean and Bob said, 'I've done most of my flying in Westchester County. That's in New York State. I'm not used to California air currents yet, especially those between Carmel here and San Francisco.'

'You really came close to that tree. I suppose they fly more flamboyantly back East. Particularly in New York. They're more liberal.'

Bob nodded slowly in the direction of the tiny loudspeaker. He tapped the side of the copter with his free hand and silver flecks came off. 'Scraped the paint a little, too. I came too close to the decorative grape arbor up on Camino Real. They shouldn't put grape arbors on top of highrise office buildings.'

'You don't understand the California mystique yet, Mr Lambrick,' replied the house. 'We're close to the earth out here, very nature-oriented. And, by the way, don't forget to wipe your feet.'

Bob noticed the clods of mud on his commute boots.

'I'll take them off and leave them out here.' He set his briefcase and portfolio down and gave a tug at one of the boots.

'Stick your feet in the bootjack,' suggested the house.

'Where is it?'

'Big cocoa-coloured box at the corner of the landing deck. You almost sideswiped it coming in. Do you always land backwards?'

Bob limped, one boot half off, to the chocolate-coloured appliance mounted at the edge of the copter area. 'I usually land the way I did today, yes. Why?'

'Oh, nothing,' said the house. 'I'm here to serve actually, not to criticize.'

Bob sat down and watched the automatic bootjack for a moment. Gingerly he opened the door and stuck one foot into the darkness. The machine whirred and chomped and yanked off his boot, his sock and part of his trouser leg. Bob said, 'I guess I don't know how to work this thing.'

'Apparently,' said the house. 'Can I give you a little advice, Mr Lambrick?'

Bob got the other boot off manually. 'Don't stop now.'

'As I say, it takes all kinds of people to make up this world of ours. Still I get the notion you're hostile to me.'

Bob stood, gathering his things. 'We've never lived in a fully automated house before.'

'Your lovely wife and yourself have been here in the Hard-castle Estates Division of Maison Technique Homes, Inc., for nearly two weeks and you, Mr Lambrick, are still ill at ease. Two weeks is rather a long spell for a shakedown cruise, if I may say so.'

'What's a shakedown cruise?'

'A nautical term. Something like a maiden voyage only in the other direction, I believe.'

'I don't know much about boats.'

'What is your profession? I mean what sort of work are you looking for?'

Bob came, partially barefooted, across the lawn. 'Public

relations. I was with a publicity outfit in New York City for three-and-a-quarter years. Now we're trying to relocate here in California.'

'I thought public relations involved getting along with people,' said the house. 'If I may say so, Mr Lambrick, you're not very affable.'

'With people I get along fine. With machines, well, it depends on the individual machine.' He reached out for the oaken door of his house.

'Let me,' said the house. The door opened automatically.

Bob came into the cocktail area sideways and dripping wet.

His wife said, 'Now what?' She was a small slender girl, with bright dark eyes and bright dark hair, twenty-seven years old.

'I was trying to take a shower before dinner,' said Bob. He was thirty, tall and about eight pounds overweight. He still had his business suit on and one sock.

'You don't take a shower,' said Hildy, 'you let the house give you one.'

'Whichever,' said Bob. 'The stall grabbed me, threw me down on the tiles and scrubbed me all over with a rough brush.'

'You must have had it set for Pets.'

'What do you mean, pets?'

'Pets. You know what pets are. Some people like to give their dogs a bath indoors now and then.'

'It didn't even wait till I got my clothes off.'

'Because dogs don't have clothes. So it's not programmed to wait.' Hildy smiled gently at her husband and then turned toward the view window. The sun was dropping, orange and bright, down to the pale blue edge of the ocean. 'Have a drink, Bob.'

'I'm soggy.'

'The laundry room will dry the suit and give you a change of clothes. I loaded it this morning.'

Bob glanced at the white door beyond the kitchen area. 'I'd rather stay soggy.'

'Bob, you're not accepting this house, are you?'

'You think I'm hostile, huh?'

'Myself, I think it's great that Pete and Alice let us sublease it while Peter's setting up that new thermal underwear factory in Brazil.'

'Um,' said Bob.

'We couldn't afford an automated, computerized house like this yet on our own budget. A lot of people even a decade older than us, and with children, can't afford a house like this.'

Bob grunted, took off his suit coat and then eased out of his wet shirt.

Hildy asked, 'Didn't you wear any underwear today, Bob?'

'No.'

'Don't you get along with your clothes closet either?'

'It gave me three pairs of shorts and a sweat sock but no T-shirt.'

Hildy smiled. 'Oh, I know why. The house thinks you'll look better, with your little paunch, wearing those new elasticized singlets. I'm going to pick up some while I'm shopping tomorrow.'

'Wait, wait,' said Bob, dropping his pants. 'The *house* thinks I'd look better?'

'It's only one man's opinion,' said the house from a speaker grid in the ceiling beam.

'Go away,' Bob shouted upwards. 'Don't interrupt.'

'He's only trying to be helpful, Bob.'

Bob said, 'Full automation, computer in the cellar, ninety-five separate appliances and servomechanisms, robot-controlled indoor environmental system, electronic entertainment system coupled with wall-size TV screen and a memory bank of three thousand classic films plus television shows from TV's golden age . . . all that I might accept. But why does he have to talk?'

'Well,' said Hildy, 'it only cost five thousand dollars more to have the house talk. This is 1985, after all, and Pete and Alice figured they . . .'

'Might as well go first-class,' Bob finished. 'Okay, Hildy. Look, would you mind taking my clothes out there to the laundry room and getting me some clean ones?'

Hildy sighed, still smiling. 'Sure, Bob. Go ahead and get a drink while I'm gone.'

'I'll have a scotch and branch water,' he said toward the portable bar.

'This is California,' said the house, as the buff-coloured bar wheeled itself over to Bob. 'How about a little Napa rosé wine instead?'

'Scotch,' repeated Bob. He sat down in his shorts and watched the sun set.

The next day, Saturday, Hildy took the copter and flew into the Carmel Valley Supermarket Complex to shop. Bob stayed at home.

At morning's end he walked cautiously into the kitchen area. He set the stove to Manual and crossed to the food compartments in the opposite wall.

'Hungover? How about a glass of tomato juice with some lime concentrate squeezed in it?' asked the house. Its speaker outlet in here was just above the sink.

'Shut up.' Bob squinted at the dialing instructions posted under the control mechanisms for the food compartments.

'How about a nice cup of mocha java?' asked the house. It chuckled. 'That's an old W. C. Fields line. You ought to be amused by that. You're always lolling around on rainy days watching old Fields movies on the TV wall.'

'Shut up.' Bob dialled two eggs and waited.

'We're all out of eggs,' the house told him. 'Hildy's got eggs at the top of her shopping list.'

Bob redialled eggs. Then he tried oatmeal. The food wall whirred and a packet of oatmeal shot out of a little door high up. Bob caught it.

'Why don't you let me fix you some hot cakes?' asked the

house. 'I've got a new recipe for Swedish-style dollar-size pancakes I'm anxious to try out. How's that sound? Swedish-style dollar pancakes, Canadian bacon and a hot cup of mocha java.'

'Shut up.' Bob pushed the dish button to the left of the sink and a platter popped up through the slot in the breakfast table.

'You have to set it for mush bowl,' pointed out the house. 'Use the dial next to the dish button.'

Bob set the dial, pushed the button. A flower-striped bowl came up through the slot and nudged the platter up and off.

After the platter had smashed on the yellow vinyl floor, the house said, 'Peter and Alice's favourite platter. Real china. I'll take care of it.'

A panel along the floor swished open and a flat vacuum rolled out. It sucked up the fragments of the smashed platter and withdrew.

Bob said, 'Thanks.' He shook the instant oatmeal into the bowl and took it to hold under the sink faucet. He slammed the hot water toggle with his free fist. Black machine oil splurted from the nozzle and onto the dry oatmeal.

'Oops,' said the house. 'You must have hit it too hard.'

Bob made a murmuring sound behind his tightly closed lips. Finally he said, 'Look, I thought you were supposed to work for me.'

'I work for the good of the house,' said the house. 'What you're hearing is the voice of the controlling computer. The type of computer used to manage each of the two dozen homes in Hardcastle Estates is of an exclusive design perfected by Maison Technique Homes, Inc. No other comparably priced home can match us.'

'So much for the commercial,' said Bob. 'Were you this nasty with Pete and Alice?'

'Nasty?' said the house from its black-and-olive kitchen grid. 'That's a matter of opinion, isn't it? What is good sense to some may seem like a vicious attack to others. Of course, Pete and Alice owned this house. That might have given them more of a sense of well-being. Ownership, I often think, cuts down on hostility.'

'I suppose Pete and Alice told you to keep an eye on me. See that I didn't botch up their house too much?'

'Of course, they are the owners and your landlords. Naturally I look out for their interests.'

'I'm paying six hundred dollars a month for this place,' said Bob. 'Six hundred dollars a month for you. So keep quiet.'

The house asked, 'Still haven't found a new job?'

'It's only been two weeks.'

'Perhaps you should have got the job first and then moved out here.'

'You sound like Hildy's father.'

'Oh? He seems like a sensible, successful man. A broker, isn't he?'

'Yes, how'd you know?'

'Hildy talks about him now and then.'

'I dón't want you to bother her when I'm at work,' Bob told the house, 'out looking for work. Another thing. Are you sure you're not monitoring us in the master bedroom?'

'Of course not. You do push your Privacy button each night?'

'Yes.'

'Then privacy is what you get. I'm only here to help.' said the house. 'Any job leads?'

'A few, but nothing concrete yet,' said Bob. 'Look, what's wrong with being adventurous when you're young? Hildy and I don't have kids yet. If I want to pick up and move to California, that's not a crime. Maybe I'll take Hildy to Spain, too, someday.'

'Do you speak Spanish?'

'No.'

'Make doing public relations in Spain difficult.'

'Maybe public relations isn't what I'll be doing all my life.'

'What else?'

'Maybe I haven't decided yet. I'm only thirty. I don't have to sign up for life right now.'

The house asked, 'Like me to fix you some breakfast?'

Bob inhaled, exhaled. Then he said, 'Okay, you might as well.' He went to the breakfast table.

The next Friday was their third wedding anniversary and Bob had a bottle of champagne under his arm along with the portfolio and attaché case when he came into the ocean-facing house late that afternoon.

Hildy was at the view window watching gulls skimming the water. 'Hi, Bob. Anything?'

Bob laughed. 'I had a pretty good interview today. With Alch & Sons. They do mostly industrial publicity, but they're a stable outfit and they pay well. I'm going back and talk to Alch himself on Monday.'

'Good,' said the pretty slender girl. 'What's that you have clutched there?'

Bob held out the bottle of champagne. 'Another piece of good luck. I found a place that stocks Taylor. So we can celebrate our anniversary with real New York champagne.'

'That stuff,' said the house.

'Shut up,' said Bob.

'I thought everybody knew,' said the house, 'that if you can't afford real French champagne you ought to choose California champagne.'

'Chauvinism on our part,' said Bob.

Hildy licked her upper lip thoughtfully. 'He's probably right, Bob. He does know a great deal about wine and food.'

'Perhaps he does,' said Bob. 'Perhaps he is indeed right. However, I am not being sentimental with this Hardcastle house. I bought this New York champagne for you and me, Hildy.' He put his things down on one of the two marble top coffee tables. 'Let's go out for dinner. Someplace on the waterfront in Monterey.'

'We've already got dinner planned,' said Hildy.

'We?'

'The house and I.'

'I hope he likes French cuisine.' The house made a lip-smacking sound.

'There must,' said Bob, 'be a way to turn him off. Not just in the bedrooms, but all over. I'm tired of him. In fact, I'm tired of this whole house.'

'You said you'd be happy in California,' said Hildy.

'I didn't know I'd be living inside a gadget.'

'Pete and Alice had other people who wanted this place,' said his wife. 'I thought you'd made up your mind you wanted an automatic house.'

'I don't know,' said Bob. 'I guess Pete talked me into it. We had to live someplace, though.'

Hildy nodded, her large dark eyes narrowing with concern. 'We can still go to Monterey for dinner. If you're not too tired after flying back and forth to San Francisco.'

Bob hesitated. 'No, that's okay. It's your anniversary, too. We'll stay home and enjoy what you've planned.'

She smiled, came to him, stretched, kissed him. 'Happy anniversary.'

'We better get started on our soufflé,' reminded the house.

Hildy kissed Bob, quickly, once more and pivoted out of his arms. Bob was still holding the bottle of New York champagne.

He was getting better at landing. Bob, grinning, hopped out of the copter and ran across the bright afternoon quarter-acre. He'd left his portfolio and briefcase on the bucket seat in the plane.

He called out, 'Hey, Hildy, good news,' as he approached the house. Then he sensed her off to his right. She was back in the sun patio, wearing a one-piece black bathing suit, sitting in a white vinyl deck chair.

She waved as he approached her. 'Early,' she said, smiling quietly, adjusting the wrap-around strip of sunglass.

'Listen,' said Bob. 'Alch & Sons came through with a great offer. They're opening a branch office in Seattle. They want me to manage it. Thirty thousand dollars a year to start.'

'I thought,' said Hildy, 'you wanted to live in California for a while?'

'I don't know,' said Bob. 'This is a good offer. They like me and I, more or less, like them.'

'Well, maybe you'll like it in Seattle.'

'You mean we'll like it.'

Hildy said, 'I don't think I want to move again. I'd like to stay here.'

'Stay here? By yourself? What do you mean?'

'Well, the house and I have done a lot of talking about this,' she began.

The Ergot Show
Brian W. Aldiss

Church interior: not very inspiring but very lofty, walls faced with mottled brown marbling, light dim, frescoes hardly recognizable. Organ case, with clock perched slenderly on its arch, is a fine and elegant work, if a little crushed between gallery and ceiling. It now peals forth with a flamboyant rendering of the toccata from Georgi Mushel's Suite for Organ, as the congregation genuflect and depart, laughing.

Pagolini emerges with his friend and fellow-artist, Rhodes, and genially rubs his hands as they descend the steps.

'A dinky service. I attend only for the sake of the departed. Things are bad enough for them without our neglect. Why should the living cut them dead? Live and let live, I say.'

He is a tall and well-built man, rugged, a very tough fifty, still with a thatch of faintly pink fair hair. Nothing eccentric, but when you've met him, you know you've met him.

Rhodes merely says, '*Coffin* is a word with a beautiful period flavour. Like *gutta percha* and *rubric*.'

Rhodes is also large, no signs of debauchery about him. He is forty-six, his face still fresh, his eyes keen behind heavy glasses. He makes love only to Thai women, and then only in the *soixante-neuf* position.

The viewpoint moves back faster than the two men move forward, revealing more and more of the church behind. It is recognizable as the Pennsylvania Station in New York, U.S.A., no longer used for rail traffic and hired by Pagolini for the occasion. The organ still plays. Most of the congregation are holding hands as they emerge, stranger smiling at stranger. There are people everywhere.

Pagolini and Rhodes cross to a public transport unit, but a moment later we see them driving across sand in Rhodes' Volvo 255S. The organ is still playing. The car filming them lies behind, occasionally drawing level for a side-shot. Some areas of the beach are crowded with people. Fortunately no-nobody is killed, or not more than one might expect.

Now the music pealing forth is – surely we recognize it with a thrill – the Byrnes Theme. 'All That We Are.' All that we are, Happened so long ago. Envelops us like a bath full of fudge.

Rhodes punches the casetteer as he steers. Naked women swim up in the holovision and dance on the dashboard. He enlarges them until they fill the windscreen and the car is zooming through their thighs. Then he flips off. 'Shall we go to Molly's as invited?'

'Feel holy enough?'

Rhodes shrugs. So Pagolini picks up the radiophone and dials Molly. Yeah, it would be dobro to see them. Come on up. Have they fixed on the two films yet? No, but they are going ahead and shooting the first one anyway. Isn't that kinda complicated? The men look at each other. 'Gutta percha, coffin, complicated', says Rhodes.

Now we are following one of Rhodes' muscle-planes as it gathers background footage over what may be regarded as a typical city of the teens of the new century: the Basque seaside tourism-and-industry centre of San Friguras. Siesta is over, the streets are crowded with people. The evening is being passed in the usual way with plenty of demo, agro, and ploto. The demo is by local trade unions demonstrating against poor working conditions and bad leisure-pay. The proto is by tourists protesting against poor holiday facilities – when you have to spend a month holidaying abroad each year to support economically depressed areas, doll, you need adequate recompense. The agro is by local yobs aggravating anyone who looks too pleased with himself.

The muscle-plane takes it all in, the five rowers straining at their wings as the cameraman, Danko Brankič, a Croat, peers through his sights. Machine-powered planes are forbidden over most Mediterranean holiday resorts. The shadow of wings flutters over the crowd. Brankič points his instrument elsewhere, eschewing obvious symbolism.

Throughout this shot, Molly is still conversing in brittle fashion over the radiophone. Despite her millions, hers is the voice of the crowd, as the demo agro proto footage may perhaps indicate.

Back-and-forth dissolve to Molly's place, where some three hundred people loll on the sunlit terraces or stroll through the shadowy rooms. She managed to pick up an old Frankfurt tube alloy factory cheap in the nineties. Gutted and plastic-lamined in black, yellow, and gamboge, it contrasts well with the replica of a Nubian palace already *in situ*.

Molly herself is rather a disappointment amid all this trendy splendour, which looks as if it were designed by Pangolini himself, although he laughed sharply when she suggested as much. The ample bust which won her the qualifying round as Mrs Ernstein-Dipthong the Third still supports her almost as well as she supports it, but the essentially shoddy bone-structure of her cheeks is beginning to show through.

We catch a guest saying, 'In five years time, give or take the give-and-take of a year either way, her chin will begin to cascade.'

A female guest replies, 'She's as high as Brankič's muscle-plane,' for all the world as if she caught the last sequence – in which we are still involved in the back-and-forth dissolve.

'*And* absorbs as much man-power.'

Molly is coming forward to greet Pangolini and Rhodes as they alight from their plane. A close-up of their expressionless faces shows rugged Adriatic scenery in the background, with the sea glinting in an old-fashioned key of blue. The camera, turning with them to greet their hostess, reveals the familiar

peak of the Matterhorn towering behind her mock-palace.
Maybe it is just a phallic symbol.

'You two gorgeous men! Things were getting just a little bit
boring until you came. Don't think I really mind but, Cecil,
do we have to have your camera team tracking you all the
time?'

'It's only my Number Two camera team,' he apologized.

'Catatonic!' she enthused.

While they are talking, the scene has been growing dark,
until it fades to a living black. No sound. An excerpt from
Jacob Byrnes' book *The Amphibians of Time* appears:

AGAIN WE FACE A TIME OF HISTORICAL CRISIS,
WHICH I CALL CLOCK-AND-GUN TIME. SUCH CRISES
HAVE OCCURRED BEFORE, NOTABLY TOWARDS
THE END OF THE THIRTEENTH CENTURY, WHEN
TOWNS WERE GROWING RAPIDLY, CREATING NEW
HUMAN DENSITIES WHICH FORESHADOWED THE
RENAISSANCE. GUNS AND CLOCKS WERE INVEN-
TED THEN, SYMBOLIZING THE OUTWARD AND
INWARD ASPECTS OF WESTERN MAN. NEW DENSI-
TIES HAVE ALWAYS CREATED NEW LEVELS OF
CONSCIOUSNESS.

A verge-escapement with foliot, ticking, ticking. Growing in
the centre of it, the ravaged and mountainous visage of Jacob
Byrnes himself.

Byrnes is talking to Rhoda, who is still in her air-drop
outfit. She brushes her hair as she listens. Hint of theme song
on a solitary violin.

'Although I could say that the globe is my habitation, I
don't share the contemporary restlessness. You know I'm
just a relic from last century, doll. But I could live anywhere,
and the Amoy ranch would suit me dandy for my declining
years. That does not bug me one bit.'

'Dobro! Then don't let it occupy you!' She still has her

superb leonine hair, unchanged now for thirty years, and it fills the screen.

'It occupies me only to this extent. Should I sell up the Gondwana estates here in the States before I move out?'

She made an impatient gesture. She loved him, had loved him, because he was not the sort of man who needed to ask questions in order to make up his mind. When he asked, it was because he had possession of the answers.

'Rhoda, you know Gondwana means a lot to me – but it is always insanity to own land. I have the essential Gondwana inside me. I'll sell – unless you want it all. If you want it all, it's all yours.'

'What about Rhodes? Is he going to film any more here?'

He crossed the room with its drab Slavonic curtains at the tall windows, he, stocky as ever, slightly too heavy. His legs were painful. He had taken to limping.

Flinging open the end door, he gestured into the writing room, which had been converted into a projection room a few months before. She looked over his shoulder.

'I know.'

Cans of holofilm were stacked here, standing on tables and floor. Some cans were not even labelled.

'Maybe they'll be back.'

She looked at him.

'No two people ever really understand each other, Jake. Give about yourself. Do you resent the tricks Rhodes and Pagolini are playing with your book?'

He grinned. 'We used to have trouble about finding where our real selves lay. Remember? That was a long time ago. We never solved the mystery. It was simply one of the fictitious problems of the twentieth century.'

'Answer my poxing question, will you?'

He picked up one of the holofilms out of the can and slid it into the projector. 'There's logic in their illogic. Even their mode of expression is outmoded now, with sense-verity arriving. So my book is doubly outmoded. At least they appear to be transmitting the basic message, that we are reaching an epoch where literacy is a handicap. Now give me a decision on what we do about Gondwana . . .'

He has flipped the power and drive switches, and the last words are played out against a three-dimensional view of the star, Quiller Singh, in a Ford-Cunard Laser 5, driving into Lhasa during the first stage of the Himalayan Rally, closely followed by two I.B.M. Saab Nanosines. Cheering lamas. A yak stampeding up a side street. Singh turns into the pits for a quick change of inertia baffles. The cube fills with bent bodies of mechanics. Steam and smoke rise in the chill sunlight.

Singh raises his goggles and looks across at Rosemay Schleiffer. Theme music, a husky voice singing, 'All that we are Happened so long ago – What we may be, That is deciding now . . .' The vantage point swings up to the monasteries clinging to battlements of the mountains and, above them on the real heights, the curly-eaved palaces of the revenant Martian millionaires.

Dissolve into interior shot of one of the curly-eaved palaces.

Antiseptic Asian light here, further bleached by hidden fluorescents. They can never get enough light, the revenants. Gravity is another matter. Old barrel-chested Dick Hogan Meyer wears reflecting glasses and leg braces, walks with a crutch attached to his right lower arm. He points the crutch at Pagolini.

'Listen to me, I may own half of Lhasa now, but when I first shipped out to Mars as a youngster, I was just a plain stovepipe welder, what they called a plainstovepipe welder. Know what that is, mister, cos they don't have them any more?'

Pagolini took a drink and said, 'Whenever you talk, Meyer, I begin to think of a certain tone of green.'

'You do? Well, you listen to me, I was one of the guys that laid the water pipes right across half of Mars, you know that?'

Very murky landscape, like a close-up shot of a boulder sparsely covered by lichen. Land and sky split the screen between them. Nothing to see except the odd crater and the depressions of the ground. Emptiness that was never filled, desolation that was always deserted. Habitable, sure, but whatever came to inhabit it would be changed in the process.

Slowly the vista moves. The machines come into view. Dexion lorries, designed to come apart and make up into different vehicles when needed. They carry giant-bore water pipes. Two excavators, a counterbalanced pipe-laying caterpillar. Down in the thousand-mile ditch, a couple of men work, welding the sleeves of the pipes together. The lorry's engine splutters, feeding in power on a thin sad note.

All the time, Dick Hogan Meyer's voice continues, although it also is thin and sad, as if attenuated by weary planetary distances.

'Men did that, working kilometre by kilometre, one hundred lengths of pipe to the kilometre. They hadn't the machines like on Earth, they hadn't the machines to do it, mister. So we did it. Mind you, the pay was great or I wouldn't have been there, would I? But, by Christ, it was hard slogging, that's what it was, mister! We lived dead rough and worked dead rough. Such a wind used to blow out of them dinky pipes, you wonder where it come from.'

'Catatonic! It's the green of a Habsburg uniform perhaps?'

'If so happen I'm boring you, you'll tell me? All I'm saying is I were just a stovepipe welder on Mars, that's how I made my jam, so what you want you'll have to spell out to me simple, so I can understand, just a simple stovepipe-welder at heart.'

Mars was gone, though still reflected in Meyer's reflecting lenses as Shackerton, smart young aide to Pagolini, came forward through the brightness of the great room saying, 'Right, right, right, Mr Meyer, me name's Provis Shackerton but never mind that – I won't bother you with irrelevancies – let's just say my name's Jones or Chang, as you prefer, and I will proceed to explain the deal in words of one syllable suited to those who carved their pile out of stovepipe-welding, right?'

He genuflected with something between a bow, a curtsey, and an obscene gesture.

'Mr Cecil Rhodes is the world's Number One film-maker, right? He is not present here. Mr Pagolini is World's Number One film-designer, right? Stands beside you. Used to be World's Number One Environment-designer, right? Designed, in fact, this Lhasa and all that therein is from what was once a fairly unpromising stretch of the Andes. Rhodes and Pagolini now work together, right? Now Mr Pagolini makes a film based loosely on the masterwork *Amphibians of Time* by Jake Byrnes – don't worry if you haven't heard of *him*, Mr Meyer, because very many rich revenant Martian stovepipe-laying millionaires are in the same ignominious position – besides he's only the greatest prophet of our pre-post-literate age – and, at the same time, Mr Rhodes will make a film of Pagolini making his film, right? All we ask of you is the loan of X million credits to recreate the 1970s, for an agreed percentage of the gross of both holofilms.'

Sneak close-up of Pagolini laughing. He adopts an English accent to say to himself, 'The poor old sod is so ignorant he thinks parthenogenesis means being born in the Parthenon.'

'Yeah, well, dobro, only what you going to do with the 1970s when you get them?' Some tendency of the old mouth to sag open. Could be the effect of Earth-gravity.

'Shoot them!' View over the busy busy idle guests. 'Shoot them all, that's what I'd like to do!' Molly says, twinkling up at the heavy glasses and the light beard of Rhodes. 'Now you come with me some place where we can talk.'

'Mind if I take a fumigant?'

'Let me show you to your suite. How about you, Pagolini, doll, darling?'

He is talking to a tall bare-bummed girl in an oriental mask, and sipping a treacly liquid through a straw. She has a straw in the same liquid and is – significantly, one supposes – not yet sipping.

'I'll be around here, Molly.'

'Cataleptic, doll!'

She takes Rhodes' arm and leads him slowly away. Dappled light and shade as of sun through lightly foliaged trees – the poplars of Provence perhaps – play over their faces as they move through the long room among the droves of elegant bodies. The expression on their faces is pleasant. Here and there, a man or woman stands naked among the other guests. One such woman is being absent-mindedly fingered by a man and wife as she plays with a little toy clown.

Molly and Rhodes enter the dance room, where strobe lights burn to the beat. The stop-start-stop-start movements of dance are abstract. Limbs are dislocated in the microseconds of dark.

'A friend of mine had epilepsy in here last week. Some sort of an illness.'

'Coffin, gutta percha, illness.'

She laughed, sagging against him. 'Dobro! Must have been hell back in the old centuries. Too few people to go round. . .'

Rhodes' beard trembles with emotion as he speaks.

'Old Byrnes was right, a true prophet. I met him – I told you, over at his ranch in the States, big ranch. Gondwana. We did some filming there. Not too good. He perceived that the essential *differentness* of humanity to other species is our inter-dependence, one on another. Sometimes we call it love, some-times hate, but it is always *interdependence*. So societies built up, always just too elaborate for the average solitary conscious-ness to comprehend. It's the building up, the *concentration*, that accounts for man's progress. We make ourselves forcing houses. Greater concentrations precede *major cultural advances*. Byrnes grasped many years ago that – '

He emphasizes what he is saying with forceful gestures, in a manner unlike his usual cool speech. He is shouting to com-pete with the insistent beat that rivals the strobes in punching sensibilities. So part of this crucial speech is lost, and is drowned out finally before completion as the camera gets snarled in dancers and loses Molly and her guest in the mêlée.

Instead we get an almost subliminal shot of Quiller Singh snarling up a series of hairpins, with Rosemay beside him in the red Laser 5.

Instead we have to put up with the bare-bummed girl smiling her beautiful best and whispering to Pagolini. 'They say she really does change her cars whenever the ashtrays are full.'

He is looking pensive. 'Probably so, but you must remember that she has cut down her smoking considerably.'

She is taking his hand and saying, 'Ride with me in an ash-tray-powered automobile and we will all the pleasures prove that stately mountain, hill, and grove. . . .'

He is running with her down a long flight of steps, saying, 'Isn't it "We with all the pleasures disprove. . ."?'

When she dives into the lake, he follows, and they sink down and down deeper, smiling at each other. All that we are Happened so long ago – What we may be . . . A cascade of harps. At the bottom of the sea, a little Greek temple with fish fluttering like birds among the pillars. They drift towards it, hand in hand.

'This is the green again, the exact green I want,' he tells her. 'We are all moving towards a new level of human conscious-ness! It's the green of *Macbeth*. You know *Macbeth*?'

'Was that the guy who swam all the way from Luna to Earth a few years back?'

'No, that was Behemoth or some such name. *Macbeth* is a Shakespeare film. That's the green I want.'

'*Rigor mortis*, man! Isn't any old green green enough?'

'Not if you are an artist. Are you an artist?'

It was all white inside the temple, white and Macbeth green. 'Ask me another.'

'Will you let me lie with you for, say, forty-three minutes?'

She looks up startled from the treacly liquid which she has now begun to sip, almost as if his fantasy disrupted her own line of thought. 'What was that?'

He stares at his watch, studying the minute, second, and

micro-second hand. 'Maybe it's not worth the bother. I was wondering if you would lie with me for around forty-one and a half minutes.'

Meyer's wife is running about the place screaming. She has a long Asian axe in her hands. A sub-title reads: LIKE AN ORDINARY AXE, BUT SHARPER. She is smashing up things.

'What is she doing?' Shackerton asks.

'She's smashing up things,' Meyer says.

'Right, right, right!' He goes over to Pagolini, who is leaning out of one of the windows looking down at the monastery roofs. 'Mrs Meyer has gone mad. Very revenant. Hadn't we better leave, right?'

'She's not mad,' Meyer explains, scratching his ear by way of apology. 'It's the ergot in the bread, that's what they tell me. Ergot in the bread – makes you mad.'

'How cataleptic to find ergot here,' Pagolini says. The view shows rows of terraced houses stretching east and west; crowning Mount Everest is a big sign reading 'LOTS', visible several hundreds of miles away – and even further than that when Earth is on the wane and you are standing in Luna City with a pair of good binoculars. 'Ergot has played a major part in influencing human history. The French character, so I have heard, has been moulded – '

'Moulded, right, right, right!' says Shackerton, screaming with laughter at the pun.

' – by various outbreaks of ergot throughout the centuries. The Ottoman Empire would have fallen two centuries before it did had not the Armies of Peter the Great, which were marching south to defeat the Turks, been afflicted by madness caused by ergot. It stopped them in Astrakhan. Make a note of that title, Shackerton – possible song there. You don't know when you are made – '

While he is speaking, Mrs Meyer has been drawing nearer, carving her way through panelling, furniture, and light fixtures as she comes.

'I know when I'm mad! And I'm good and mad now!'

'Right, right, right!'

'Catatonic!'

'She does know, too, she does!'

Meyer runs to a huge gamboge sofa that would hold ten, swivels it round, and reveals an escape chute. They take it. Mrs Meyer comes after them, axe in hand. As they pick themselves up in the snow, she runs past them and begins to chop up the Pagolini helicopter.

'She likes a good whirley-bird when the fit takes her, does my Mary,' Meyer says, with just a touch of complacency to his sorrow.

'Coffin, complicated, gutta percha, whirley-bird,' collects Pagolini. He appears somewhat impatient.

'Figgle-fam, then,' says Meyer, sulkily. He is caught at a disadvantage. He goes over to where one of the rotor vanes lies, stoops, holding the small of his back as he bends, and retrieves a shattered vane.

'I suppose I'd better agree to financing the 1970s,' he says. People can change Without any why or how, Powers will emerge Building behind your brow . . .

The axe comes flying and catches Shackerton on the glutea maxima. He falls, screaming.

Blood fills the screen. A notice appears:

FOR THE BENEFIT OF THOSE WHO WOULD CARE TO LEAVE THIS
THEATRE NOW

It hangs there in the void before giving way to its completion, and the dissolve is so slow that the two ends of the sentence intermix irritatingly before the end can be read.

FOR THE BENEFIT OF THOSE WHO WOULD CARE TO LEAVE
WE ANNOUNCE THAT THE REST OF THE FILM IS
THIS THEATRE NOW
NON-VIOLENT

The screams of Shackerton fade as the theme emerges again.

WE ANNOUNCE THAT THE REST OF THE FILM IS NON-VIOLENT

'Isn't it a bit of a muddle?', Rhoda asked, as Byrnes switched off.

'Life?'

'The Rhodes epic.'

'To a degree.'

'Come on, Jake. It's a load of bullshit!'

'Life?'

'He isn't making one connection with your book, not one little connection, right?'

'Right, right, right!' He laughed. 'Let's go and get an old-fashioned alcoholic drink, the kind that these holofilm guys don't use any more.'

As they padded back into the rather old-fashioned living area, where an alligator dozed with open eyes beside an ivory pool, he said, 'No, honey, Rhodes has made the connection okay. He is second generation to my book. He finds the book kind of fuddy-duddy simply because the message got across to him so long ago that he acts on it well nigh instinctually.'

She smiled, curling her long legs beneath her as she settled by the pool and started fondling the drugged reptile. ' "Well nigh." Coffin, gutta percha, what was the other thing?'

'*Literacy*. The mass-psychosis of the 1970s was merely build-up for the break-through into a higher level of human consciousness. That's what we're witnessing now. Rhodes' epic would hardly be intelligible a few years ago. And he has seen that literacy has to go, just as I predicted.'

She accepted the drink he poured her and set the clouded glass down on the alligator's head.

'You explained to me before about why literacy has to go, but I still don't get it. It's to do with needing more dimensions, isn't it?'

'The linear business, yes. More importantly, we are going to regain senses by sloughing off literacy. Those who could write ruled the world for – what? – ten thousand years. Very powerful minority, but only a minority in almost any culture you care to name. They were the clerks, and they shaped civilization. Now Rhodes, and more especially the generation after him – the true inheritors of this alien new century – they are shaking off the stultifying effects of literacy and getting back all the senses that have to be sacrificed to master a printed page and the cultures of the printed page.'

Rhoda sipped her drink and then began to slide into the pool.

'And this sloughing of literacy, as you call it, is the result of computerization?'

'I'd put it this way, and how lovely you look! – The result of man's still-developing mind. We have never been satisfied with our limited senses. The earliest men painted and developed weapons to extend their psychespheres. But some senses we were born with got lost in the upward battle, just as Meyer lost all potentiality in his fight for brute cash. Now that computers take most of the load, we reclaim many old freedoms. . .'

She smiled up at him as he stripped.

'You hairy old ape! Come in with me. Drag Horace in!'

'You and I, Rhoda, my eternal love, we are the first man and woman on this planet.' And he blundered down into the water beside her.

'Ah, the female element!'

The Number Two camera crew are sitting on the wide landing outside Rhodes' suite, drinking stepped-milk and eating chickwiches. The landing is lumbered with Molly's signature motifs, bright and outrageous confections inspired by Khmer art, burial ornaments, and the morphology of insects. The boys munch and chatter.

'Wonder how Danko and his gang are getting on . . .'

'Yeah . . .'

'Think they'll let us sleep here?'

'You know the Commo-capitalist system, boy – you'll be sacking out on the beach tonight.'

'What beach? The mountains, you mean!'

'Get phased! You're on the wrong dinky set.'

'Alpha, I was getting muddled . . .'

'What's she doing in there with Cecil, anyway? Not being Thai, she'll get no change out of him!'

Beyond his moving mouth, before the chickwich comes up again, we see the door open and Molly emerge. We glide through the door before she can close it.

Rhodes is polishing his spectacle lenses; without them, he has a deceptively mild look.

'Gun-and-Clock Time . . .'

He kicks off his boots.

There is an array of screens in the hall of his suite. He pads over to them and turns them on. Views of packed humanity everywhere, long distance or swooping to close-up revealing skin texture as he twiddles the controls. He fiddles the volume at the same time, so that noise comes and goes. We see Meyer running through the snow, weeping, pursued by his wife who still wields the axe. Shots from Pagolini's fantasy, swimming down to the temple – what he dreamed, someone else acted out in reality because the Earth is so crowded that coincidence is one with coffin and complicated. Shots of Danko Brankič sill flying noiselessly in and out of choking Mediterranean alleys. Byrnes, belly upwards, floating beside an alligator and a blonde. Quiller Singh, his Laser 5 belting triumphantly into Katmandu.

Rhodes laughs.

'Great old prehistoric man, Byrnes! We've left him behind. Left them all behind . . . New human beings are coming up.'

Flicking over switches with decision, he hurries back into the adjoining room among plastic insect bodies and adjusts monitor and scanner so that he can stand and see himself burning solid in the screen. He begins to 'act,' reciting rather than speaking.

'Earth swarms with people – crawls with people. It's full up with people, but there's still room for more. Byrnes saw it first – this film is our tribute to him while he still lives. He saw that the population explosion was a positive thing, born from our love of children, of more and more life. He saw that great pressure of population was necessary for man to be forced into his next stage of being, a new level of awareness, a greater integration. From the mass-psychosis of the twentieth century, a new sanity is being born. Now that we have entire control of population-build-up, and can feed our glad new mouths, we need fear nothing except the old fears . . .'

Then he burst out laughing.

'Cut! I'm talking twentieth-century rhodomentade! One foot in the past, that's me – but we'll get there. One more generation, psyche striking sparks off psyche . . . It needs seeing . . .'

His voice tails off inaudibly. He goes over to the interior omnivision and switches on. Room after room is revealed, many untenanted, many bare of furnishing. Some are packed with human activity. He hits on one room where there is a monitor screen burning. He sees himself in it.

The woman viewing his image looks up, startled but smiling. She waves, her lips move, but Rhodes has the volume too low to hear. He flicks on. He is searching searching for a nest of Thai girls. Molly must have one somewhere in her castle.

He flips on to the terraces, zooms in on Pagolini just getting up to go, holding the hand of his bare-bummed girl.

'Ever see a movie called *Kid Auto Races at Venice*?'

'Is that a movie?'

'Quite an historic one.'

Rhodes is fiddling with the volume. Their voices are enormously loud, echoing through the room, growing louder as Pagolini and the girl retreat from the eye of the camera.

Pagolini is talking to Byrnes and Rhoda in a cathedral. They walk up and down. It is an unusual cathedral, very heavy – possibly the cathedral in Saragossa, Spain.

'This is where we intend to start recreating the 1970s. This cathedral is not used any more, except for the benefit of

tourists – they get about fifty thousand through the turnstiles
on an average day in the high season. I have bought it. A
performance of *Macbeth* was given here some years ago which
I stage-managed. I like the colouring.'

'Maybe we should holiday near here and watch you shoot,'
Rhoda said.

'You know what a Macbeth green is?'

'Sure, it's the place where the witches three shacked up.'

'You are a lady of the old culture.'

'You must get in my point about cities as a symbol of the
death of the old human psyche, Signor Pagolini. The Roman-
tics are the sickening point. Their cities slowly sink underground. Remember Kublai Khan's pleasure dome, and the
subterranean passages in Poe . . . Partly they were the effect of
opium, but only in part.' As he speaks, he stops to study some
intricate stucco ornamentation, not noticing that Pagolini
has walked on with Rhoda. 'In later writers, the psyche fades
lower still. The writings of Cocteau and Asimov provide
examples. Asimov has whole underground planets, if one may
so say . . . Psychic death before rebirth. Dark before renaissance . . .'

There is a beautiful shot of Pagolini and Rhoda as they
pause far down the patterned aisle under the high windows.
She hesitates, as if wishing to go back to Jake. Jake's voice is
lost. Before Pagolini can turn to her, a girl appears in the
main entrance, framed in light from outside. She may be the
girl he is later to discover on Molly's terraces. She wears a
long simple dress of frail material which might have been
designed from a Walter Crane drawing. When Pagolini sees
her, he in his turn hesitates, looking back to see what Rhoda is
doing. People caught in light, transfixed, transformed. All this
in long shot, viewed from Byrnes' pillar.

Rhoda makes a slight gesture. Pagolini interprets it as one
of assent. With a slight bow to her, he turns towards the door,
the daylight, the girl framed there. Beyond her, the crowded
square can faintly be discerned. The camera crew is there,

ready to record the moment of splendour when Pagolini emerges. Is that Rhodes, sitting on a camera dolly?

The organ is playing part of Georgi Mushel's Suite for Organ – something of a second-rate piece of music.

Almost subliminal shot of Pagolini manifesting himself in the doorway from outside. The cathedral is Pennsylvania Station.

Another cathedral façade – or at least a monstrous building. Shadow of the muscle-plane over it. The plane lands. While the five rowers slump over their oars, Rhodes and Brankič jump nimbly out.

Rhodes walks along the promenade by the sea, head down, hands clasped behind his back in a somewhat dejected fashion.

DON'T WORRY – ALL ENDS HAPPILY

Brankič trudges behind, lugging cans of film.

OR CEASES ON A NOT UNHAPPY NOTE, LET'S SAY

'We also have to bring in the dear departed. Where would we all be without the countless past generations copulating away for our sakes?'

Brankič chuckles. 'You don't really want to make a holo. You want to recreate life itself.'

Rhodes also chuckles. 'Right, right, right!' he quotes.

On the snow-covered cliffs above them are running figures. We see Mrs Meyer, axeless now that the madness has passed. She weeps as she flees, pursued by her husband, who is wielding the axe. Some day we'll evolve so far, we'll become All That We Are . . . Louder and louder, till drowned by the ticking of a clock. Last chance to study a verge-escapement with foliot before the house-lights come up.